D0873684

LOST IN THE OUTBACK

Newly qualified teacher Amy Shaw has a lot of adjusting to do when she moves from Sydney to remote Gurawang. On her first night there, someone plants an explosive in a railway wagon outside her hotel window — the first in a chain of dramatic events that colour Amy's new life. After a nearly catastrophic misstep with a handsome local banker, does she have a chance at winning the heart of the town's senior constable — and can they work together to dispel the shadows that hang over Gurawang?

ALAN C. WILLIAMS

LOST IN THE OUTBACK

Complete and Unabridged

LINFORD
Leicester

First published in Great Britain in 2018

First Linford Edition
published 2020

A catalogue record for this book is available
from the British Library.

ISBN 978–1–4448–4401–6

Published by
F. A. Thorpe (Publishing)
Anstey, Leicestershire

Set by Words & Graphics Ltd.
Anstey, Leicestershire
Printed and bound in Great Britain by
T. J. International Ltd., Padstow, Cornwall

This book is printed on acid-free paper

1

I gazed at the almost deserted main street of Gurawang. Even though it was the beginning of 1970 and not 1870, it still looked like the Aussie equivalent of a wild-west ghost town.

'What's going through that pretty head of yours, Amy?' Frank asked as he stopped his car outside the Railway Hotel. It had been a long, hot, often dusty trip from Sydney to my new home; three hundred and thirty miles over the Blue Mountains and across swathes of wheat fields or pastures the colour of butter, only the occasional flock of Merinos showing there was life in the bush.

'I'm scared . . . well, apprehensive. I'm on my own for the first time in my life. All those years of wanting my own space. Now I'm remembering that saying, *be careful what you wish for.*

Sure you don't fancy a drink before you get going?'

Frank looked at his watch. He still had a two-hour drive to reach his own new school. We'd been in the same class at teaching college and though there were only fourteen of us, we'd never been close; he was five years older than I was. In any case, he'd already been kind enough to drive me here despite Gurawang being out of his way.

I glanced at the signs advertising beer on the outside of the building. My legs were aching from the drive. Stretching, we ambled over to a wide veranda that gave some shelter from the ninety-degree sun. Country pubs were so different to city ones, their broken-tiled facade always reminding me of the inside of public toilets.

Noticing a *Missing* poster tacked to the wooden wall, I went to read it.

'Seems like some boy disappeared just before Christmas. Nine years old.'

'Bad things happen everywhere, Amy. Not just in the Big Smoke.'

'Out here it seems more real. I guess the whole town knew him. Probably went to my school.'

The grainy picture was of a cheeky face, smiling for some family photo. Poor kid. Poor family.

'I'll help you take your bags in, though I do have to get going, Amy. It'll be night at eight o'clock and I don't fancy hitting a roo in the dark on these roads. We have each other's addresses. It's not as if you'll be teaching in some foreign country.'

I pointed to a painted notice by the front door.

No sheilas in the main bar. Ladies' Salon first door on the left.

'Sure about that, Frank?' I gave a wan smile.

'You'll be OK, kid. From what I hear, they look after their schoolies in these outback towns.'

Although he was only slightly taller than me, he was strong enough to easily lift out the boxes and cases packed into Susie Q, his 1963 EJ Holden station wagon. This morning it had been two-toned grey and white. That had changed to grey and Aussie dust-brown. Splattered insects smeared the front wind-shield and bonnet.

I was reluctant to say goodbye to the last contact of my past.

'Why do you reckon they'd care for a new teacher, then?' I asked.

Frank brushed his hair back from his perspiring forehead. 'Gene pool. They need new blood to keep the local population from getting too inbred.'

I shuddered. No way was Amy Shaw marrying a local cockie to spend her life on a sheep ranch!

'Thanks so much for that parting thought, Frank. I'll have nightmares for the next month.'

As if on cue, a ute pulled up across the road. Two young blokes jumped out, laughing and joking. They were wearing tattered blue jeans with Aussie Akubra hats. As they passed on their way to the pub, one tipped his hat to me. I nodded politely, realising the smell of sheep that suddenly assaulted my senses was coming from them.

'Look on the positive side, Amy,' said Frank with a wink. 'Marry one of them and you'll not only have a tractor for every day of the week but a good two acres of topsoil.'

I giggled. 'Frank. I'll miss those jokes of yours.'

There was an awkward pause.

'Appreciate you paying for Susie Q's petrol and our lunch. 'Sides, it was great to have company. Just give you a hand lugging this lot into the hotel.' He hefted a case, almost dropping it on his foot. 'Sure there isn't a kitchen sink in here?'

I stared at my two bags of clothes and toiletries plus my reel-to-reel tape recorder with all my music tapes copied from my records. The sound was loads better than those cassette players. Then there were my teaching folders and text books. Frank's station wagon was looking decidedly empty after my possessions were taken out. Men travelled a great deal more lightly.

As we walked into the dingy reception, I had to remove my sunnies. The air stank of cigarette smoke and cheap room freshener. And sheep.

'Thanks for everything, Frank. Take care.'

'Will do. You know me. A girl in every port.' It was a standard joke; the class knew he had no luck with women. He was five foot six and quite stocky — not the usual image of a bronzed Aussie male. Hopefully he'd find a woman in Jerilderie whom he could love and who'd love him in return.

I reached to shake his hand, then decided a hug was more appropriate. As he walked back to Susie Q, I was reminded that this was the start of my working life, miles from everyone I knew.

In spite of being twenty years old, I realised I was pretty naïve. Dad's comment of being thrown in at the deep end was a definite understatement.

School started on Tuesday. It was

Saturday tomorrow. Sunday, everything would be closed, as it would on Monday's holiday. Two hundred years since Captain Cook sailed into Botany Bay.

I glanced at the hotel reception's notice board.

Australia Day party night, 1970, was the poorly written sign pinned to the cork. Another Missing leaflet was next to it.

The outside door opened and Frank appeared.

'Amy. Looking around here, you really do need to buy a car. You'll be stuck without it.'

'Yeah. Need to start earning money first, sport. Not everyone is as rich as you.'

★   ★   ★

I rang the reception bell twice without any response. Finally I called 'Cooee' and a tubby older bloke came through a door from the noisy bar area. His black

7

hair and beard were short, with bushy eyebrows to match. He mopped his forehead with a towel that had seen better days.

'Yeah. What do you want, girlie?'

I wasn't used to being called girlie. The last male who did was Neil Simpson back in fourth class. I'd laid him out with a right uppercut. I'd been lectured by Mr Christie, the headmaster, about self-restraint and unladylike behaviour, but the boys gave me a wide berth after that.

I considered doing the same to this bloke before deciding against it. No point in antagonising the locals on my first day, or getting a reputation as a carrot-top with an attitude problem. Also he was probably the landlord of the hotel I needed to stay in until I could find permanent accommodation.

'G'day. I'm Amy Shaw. I have a room booked.'

A middle-aged lady entered, wiped her hands on her apron and walked up to me.

'Ah yes. Miss Shaw. Been expecting you. I'll take over, Jimmy. You get back to your two-up.'

Jimmy grunted before returning to the bar.

'I thought two-up was illegal,' I said without thinking. The traditional Aussie gambling game betting on which sides two pennies landed was less popular in the big cities.

'Depends if you play for money,' she replied with a wink. 'I'm Doreen, the landlady here. You the new schoolie?'

'Is it that obvious?'

'It's a small community here. Having a new teacher is big news. I'll help you with your bags.' She looked at my array of luggage. 'On second thoughts, I'll get my son to lend us a hand.'

With that she bellowed his name. A teenage boy came through from the back, suddenly breaking into a smile when he saw me. Young boys and their hormones! I wondered if he'd be one of my new students. Doreen introduced him as Glen.

Between the three of us, we made it upstairs to a double room overlooking a single railway line. There was nothing else visible beyond, apart from a metal closed-in wagon on a siding a hundred or so yards off. After that, all I could make out was barren ground and barbed wire fences. Not exactly a room with a view.

'Bathroom's down the hall. Don't worry about privacy. You're it for tonight. Gurawang ain't one of the most popular places on the tourist route.'

The room was clean but dated. The peeling striped wallpaper somehow complemented the sash window with its torn fly-screen stretched across the wooden frames. The bed sheets were relatively clean and ironed, although that faded green chenille bedcover would be put aside the minute Doreen left. It was a relic from the fifties.

Doreen switched on the bedside fan with its rust-tinged blades. It did nothing except circulate the stifling air from one side of the room to the other. Two fly-papers wafted to and fro. I tried to ignore the carcasses of blow-flies stuck there.

'Got a car, Amy? Park out the back if you want.'

'No. No car. Isn't there public transport here?'

'Nearest station is Leeton, 'bout forty minutes' drive, and no buses 'cept the school ones.'

'What about that railway line?' I asked. 'Plus you are called the Railway Hotel.'

'Solely for freight. Wheat trains. Not so many these days. If I was you I'd get a car, quick smart.'

'Yeah. I've been told that already. Thanks.'

Glancing outside I noticed a moustached figure over near the railroad truck. He kept glancing behind as if concerned about being seen. Stranger still was his heavy coat and hat. In this weather, it must have been uncomfortable.

'Doreen. Should that guy be lurking out there?'

'What bloke, dearie?'

He'd disappeared from sight.

'Doesn't matter.'

She didn't seem bothered. In fact her entire manner was indifference, as though she was simply going through the motions.

In the darkened hallway Doreen gave me the room key.

'Meal times is six to eight. Nothing fancy but I can guarantee a decent helping.'

I spied yet another of those *Missing* posters on the wall. Doreen saw me notice it.

'Our youngest, Graham. Big search at the time, police plus all the townsfolk from hereabouts. Can't understand what happened to him. One minute he was with his friends, playing down at the creek. The next . . . ' She stifled a sob. 'They had one of those helicopters from Wagga Wagga they use with bushfires. Spent days searching.'

Her face said it all. No wonder. She wanted Graham back more than anything and her life without him was empty.

'Jimmy says I should take them down. Says I should accept he ain't coming back. But . . . I can't. Not ever. If someone might see that photo and has any idea where my boy is, then that's a good thing. That's why I've left all those posters up in the town. Just in case.'

As her breathing started to become erratic, she took out an inhaler from her apron but managed to control herself without using it.

'Asthma,' she explained. 'Talking about Graham sets it off some days.'

All I could think of were empty platitudes. I'd never lost anyone close. At that moment I realised just how much growing up I still needed to do.

A shout from her husband caused her to scurry downstairs, leaving me with my thoughts. I couldn't imagine how I'd feel if my younger brother or either of the twins went missing.

I locked my room door. Over a month since Graham vanished, just after the summer holidays started. I wondered if I could help in any way — even simply as someone to listen. It seemed Jimmy wasn't there when Doreen needed him. Tomorrow we could have a natter, if she wanted.

Right now, I wanted to kick off my sandals and relax. There was a jug of lukewarm water on the Queen Anne dressing table along with a glass with a Resch's Beer label transferred on. They had embroidered doilies weighted down by beads draped over their tops to keep the flies away.

My old high school had been next to the Resch's Brewery in Sydney. A vision sprang to mind; afternoons studying maths with Mrs Bradford while the whiff of brewing hops bathed the room. We might have been too young to drink alcohol then, but we reckoned we could still breathe it in.

The quicksilver coating on the mirror

was flaking in places. Still, I didn't expect more. I'd seen a lot of country pubs on trips with Mum and Dad. Stayed in a few too, despite Mum preferring those new motels springing up. She insisted they were cleaner. Pity there wasn't a motel here.

Four days until my first day as a teacher. I wondered what the other staff and kids would make of me. The mirror should've shown a classy Aussie woman, ready to take on the world, yet all I could see was curly copper hair falling loosely over some kid's freckled face.

I sighed. *Sophisticated? In your dreams, Amy.*

I was five foot four and, as my less friendly schoolmates had told me, 'a skinny little runt'. During the last few years, I'd matured from skinny little runt to skinny slightly-taller runt.

Dad had often told me, 'Amy. You gotta believe in yourself and ignore what those other girls say.' *Easy for him to say*, I thought at the time. It was only later that I realised he'd had a tough life too. I wished he was here right now.

At least the wardrobe had a few hangers for my frocks. I didn't want them wrinkled. Impressions would be important on my first day teaching.

I held my best dress in front of me, posing.

'Hello, class. I'm Miss Shaw, your new science teacher,' I said aloud with all the conviction I could. It had a beaut sound to it.

The hotel was hopefully just for tonight. Tomorrow, first priority would be to find a more stable place to stay. I didn't fancy being here for too long. I couldn't even have an alcoholic drink . . . well, not legally. Minimum age for drinking was twenty-one in New South Wales. I thought it was the same in Victoria, which was two hours' drive by car. Yeah. A car. Definitely had to buy one.

As it was after five, the shops would be shut. Anyway I was bushed from the drive. I lay down on the mattress, expecting a broken spring or two. There didn't seem to be any living flies nearby, and thankfully no filthy cockroaches. Despite me being a science teacher, they freaked me out.

Reaching into my handbag, I took out my writing pad and a Bic. I'd promised Mum I'd write when I arrived. Until I could set up a bank account here, I'd have to rely on my cash. I checked my purse. Ninety-seven dollars and thirty-five cents. Fingers crossed, it would be enough.

I chewed the end of my blue pen. Dad would tell me off for that. There wasn't a great deal to write. After all, I'd seen them this morning.

Once I'd finished, I read a detective novel for a bit; that prompted me to remember the guy I saw earlier. Why had he been behaving so furtively? Checking from my window, there was no one in sight. That was a good thing.

★   ★   ★

Tea was tasty yet uneventful. I spoke only to Doreen. There was no one else in the Ladies Salon, naturally; just when I felt like a bit of a chinwag. Another thing I'd have to get used to; back home, teatime discussions of the day's events were the norm. I even missed Peter's whingeing about having to eat all his veggies.

Deciding on an early night, I had a shower down the hall and settled in.

Around quarter past two I woke up. Maybe it was the heat, or some noise. The hands of my travel alarm clock were glowing faintly and I could just see the moon's crescent through the window.

I listened for movement in the hall or nearby rooms. Nothing. No barking dog or stupid rooster whose own alarm had gone off early.

Then I heard it; footsteps on the gravel of the railway track. They stopped as I pushed myself from the creaky bed to have a peek.

At first I saw no one. A few seconds

passed before a silhouette moved from the shadows into the moonlit area beneath me. All I could see was a figure dressed darkly, carrying a large bag. He was obviously adult and up to no good, judging by his stealthy movements.

All of a sudden, as if sensing my presence, he stared straight at me just as the moonlight emerged from behind a cloud. Was he the same man I'd noticed earlier? He was already legging it down the curving tracks as fast as he could, disappearing past the hotel corner.

I went to turn on the light, walking away from the window. Suddenly everything lit up and I was hurled across the room as an explosion shattered the window. My ears were ringing, and pain racked my body where I'd been thrown against the wall.

What the ... ? I thought, groaning. Opening my eyes a little I saw flames dancing on the shards of glass scattered everywhere.

I struggled to understand what was happening.

I needed to get to safety. Unfortunately, every movement I made to sit up caused me to wince.

At least nothing seemed broken. Then I felt the wetness covering my arms and legs.

It must be my blood. I'd been injured. And there was no one there to help me.

2

I yelled out. No one answered, so I listened. There were no screams or crying or calls for help. Then I recalled I was the only guest. The pub owners lived in another part of the building.

Pulling myself up carefully, I managed to flip the light switch. I breathed a sigh of relief as I saw it wasn't my blood that covered me. It was the water from the broken jug.

Glass covered my bed and the floor to one side of the room. Fortunately there was none near me. It must have been one massive explosion . . . bottled gas or petrol maybe.

I stood there in shock, trying to take it all in. The pain was lessening. The impact had certainly knocked the stuffing out of me.

In a daze I edged to the window, avoiding the glass on the threadbare rug. The railway truck was gone, blasted apart. Patches of burning debris littered the tracks as well as the side of a brick building just visible to my right. It had taken the brunt of the blast. The galvanised iron roof and its supporting timbers had collapsed in places.

Footsteps running up the stairs jolted me from my stunned state. 'Amy. Are you all right?' shouted Doreen from outside my door.

'Yes. I think so,' I replied in a hoarse whisper. I repeated myself louder as I turned the key.

She had a thin dressing gown and slippers on. I realised my nightie was all I was wearing.

'Quick. My daughter!' Doreen was frantic.

'What about Jimmy?'

'Not here. Only you. Hurry.'

Slamming on my sandals, I dashed after her as fast as my battered body would let me.

We ran down the stairs, turning left into a narrow passageway leading to the family annex. I figured help was on its way. There'd be the volunteer fire brigade and the cops at least. Luckily the ceiling lights were working.

'Move it, Amy. I can't open her door.'

As we ran, brick walls replaced wooden ones. Doreen pointed to a door up ahead.

'That's Sharon's room. Sharon . . . Sharon. Can you hear me, love?'

The door was jammed shut. Doreen's breathing was becoming more difficult.

She called out while I shoved the solid door. It budged a little, then stopped. Peering through the gap, I could see fallen timbers.

'Mummy. I'm scared,' a tiny voice answered before bursting into a coughing fit.

'We're coming, darling. Mummy's coming.'

'What about the window?'

'No good. Bars,' she explained.

'You put your daughter in a barred room?'

'It's the old bank!' she screamed. 'If I

had . . . any idea . . . ' Her voice trailed off into laboured breathing.

That explained the brick walls. Had to be the door, then. I had to calm down for Sharon's sake.

'Doreen. Do you have a fire axe?'

'An axe? I'll get it.'

Everything seemed stable for now; however those tin roofing sheets were heavy and with sharp edges. The faster she got out, the better.

At that moment, I caught the smell of something apart from the dust. Smoke? There was burning and it seemed to be in Sharon's room. Curls of greyness rose from the gap under the door and through the space I'd forced open.

Doreen returned in seconds, her rapid gasping telling me that she was struggling.

'Is that smoke?' she asked.

Grabbing the axe, I nodded.

'My God. There's a fire. You have . . . you have to get her . . . '

'I will. You have to leave, Doreen. Your asthma.'

She stood crying and wringing her hands. Her eyes were wide in terror.

I grabbed the heavy axe and began swinging at the door. Already I could feel the heat and hear the crackling of burning wood. I realised how badly injured I was. Doreen's distraught behaviour was understandable, but right now, it was a major distraction. I had to focus on the door.

'Doreen! Get outside. I'll save Sharon but I can't carry you out too. I'll save her.'

Precious seconds went by. Another swing. I turned to glare at her, wiping perspiration on my sleeve. The damned door seemed to be made of Tassie oak. Each blow reverberated through my body, and my arms and shoulders ached. I couldn't make headway and the smell of smoke was stronger. We were both finding it hard to breathe. Decision time.

'Doreen! Go! You have to go! Now!'
Tears filled her eyes.
'I can't lose her too. I . . . I can't.'

'Then for God's sake. Trust me . . . Please.'

Finally she turned away, stumbling along the corridor. Outside there was the sound of sirens.

The solid panel began to splinter as the door and frame shifted. Simultaneously, the lights began to flicker. I prayed they'd keep going long enough for me to grab Sharon.

'Break . . . ' One more blow.

'You . . . ' And another.

'Bloody door.'

The axe crashed through, smashing the door apart far enough for me to climb through.

Finally. Grunting with the effort, I shoved the timbers to one side with my shoulder, hoping that it wouldn't bring the ceiling crashing down on us.

'Mummy! Hurry!'

Smoke billowed before clearing enough for me to see Sharon crouched in a corner by her bed. She was coughing, hands held over her mouth. Her eyes were closed. The acrid fumes must have been stinging them. She opened her eyes to see me, then stared mesmerised by the dancing flames lapping the far wall up to the ceiling. She curled up tighter.

'Hold your breath, Sharon. I'm coming.'

Her little arms reached out. Thank goodness for that. My nightie caught on a jagged beam as I scooped her into my arms. I had to get outside.

I staggered back down the corridor, Sharon's tiny arms clasped around my neck. Part of the ceiling gave way behind us, taking the failing lights with it. It wasn't pitch black, yet it made our progress a lot slower.

There were more sirens, and flashing lights were visible through the windows ahead. The ground floor of the older part of the hotel seemed intact. The lights there were a welcome sight.

A man was racing towards us with a fire blanket that he draped around us. I was grateful as, even though my modesty remained intact, I felt exposed in my torn and soot-covered nightwear.

Understanding that she was now safe, Sharon smiled at me; our faces almost touching.

'You said the B word.'

'Yes, sweetie. I suppose I did,' I replied, feeling the tension leaving me. I ached everywhere but Sharon was safe. I couldn't believe it. She was safe. And I did it.

Once out in the clear air, Doreen ran forward to embrace us both. I passed Sharon to her.

'Thank you, Amy. Thank . . . thanks so much. I . . . I don't know what to say.'

More volunteer firemen arrived, moving towards Sharon's room where the devastation was clearly evident. Flickers of tangerine and yellow flames illuminated the damaged structures.

We eased Sharon down onto a bench. Although she was still coughing, her breathing was becoming deeper and more regular. A guy appeared telling me he was a doctor and immediately assumed control. That gave me a chance to step back and wrap the blanket round me properly.

All around, people and cars arrived. I simply watched the drama unfold. I was totally drained and bruised from the ordeal; I'd done my bit. A police car roared up, followed ten minutes later by an ambulance.

Someone then parked a tractor so that the whole scene was lit up by its powerful lights. The stark, elongated shadows were so alien, although the wisps of smoke from the fires were dissipating now that the fire guys had the pumps going. There was shouting from every side but all I could manage was to stare at the water pooling on the Tarmac on the pub car park.

My clothes and possessions were in that ruined bedroom. It made a traumatic night far, far worse. This was not what I'd imagined the first night in my new home town was going to be like.

The light from the tractor was

blocked out by a man standing over me.

'Who are you, Miss? What are you doing here?' he asked. The voice was deep and official, without a trace of compassion.

I was too tired for twenty damn questions. Too tired and only now registering that if I'd been in front of my window when it was blown apart, I'd have been seriously injured.

'Get lost. Go bother someone else,' I replied.

'Hold on, lady. This is a criminal enq — '

'She's the new school teacher, Kyle. She saved my Sharon. Leave her alone, she's had a bad night.' It was Doreen.

'Even so, I need some answers, Doreen. A railway wagon blows up, destroying property and injuring people in my town.'

His town? What sort of arrogant bloke . . . ? He stood to one side, allowing me to see his boots and uniform. A copper. That figured. Although I respected the police, we were brought up to be wary of them. Unlike cops like on that Pommie TV show, *Z-Cars*, Aussie police were generally standoffish, rude, and armed. Also the men were built like rugby players — tall, beefy and thick as a brickie's sandwich.

Gurawang's officer was no different, it seemed. In the macabre lighting I could see he was probably in his mid-twenties with short dark hair. He sat down next to me on the bench, jarring me slightly. I edged away from him.

'Sorry, Miss. I'm Senior Constable Travis, Kyle. I need help and it seems you were in the hotel when it all kicked off. While I understand you're upset, I need an idea why that wagon blew up.'

OK. Maybe I was wrong about the rude part. And he was simply doing his job.

'There . . . was someone nearby just before. I saw him. Think it was a bloke. He had a large bag stuffed with something. Ran off when he noticed me. He'd broken into the wagon. The door was open now I think about it.'

'Thanks, Miss . . . '

'Amy.'

'Thanks, Amy. I guess he's long gone by now. Nice dressing gown, by the way.' He smiled.

'Not the word I'd use.' I grinned. 'Didn't think that coppers were allowed to smile.'

'Only on Australia Day weekend. Has the doc seen you yet?' I shook my head. 'Doc. Over here when you're ready.'

'Coming, Kyle. Sharon's ready to go with the ambulance to Leeton. Are you going with her, Doreen?' The doctor was definitely a Pom.

'Too right, Mac. You make sure you sort out this girlie too. She's a heroine.'

Kyle stood so that the doctor could sit. Then the policeman switched on his torch, momentarily blinding me. I saw the state of my hands and guessed the rest of me looked worse as both the doctor and Kyle took deep breaths.

'Have I messed up my lippy?' I joked

before unexpectedly bursting into tears.

'Let's get her inside. I'll sort her out with some sweet tea. Some for all of us, I reckon.' Suddenly Kyle's broad Aussie accent seemed so comforting.

At that moment a ute with spotlights on the roof braked to a screeching halt in front of us. Jimmy and his son, Glen, jumped out.

'Holy dooley, Doreen! What's going on?' he demanded, brusquely.

'What's going on, Jimmy, is that someone's destroyed part of the pub, your little girl's been in a fire and I'm off to hospital with her. I'll leave it to you to sort it all out.'

'Me? But . . . '

'Yes, you. You're off chasing blinking foxes when you should have been here. Move Amy into the family room and cook her a decent brekkie. She saved Sharon tonight.'

Suddenly I saw a different side of Doreen — one that scared Jimmy. It looked like I'd have a room instead of a bomb-site for the night after all.

As Doreen clambered into the ambulance she called out, 'Oh, Jimmy — better phone that waste-of-space insurance mate of yours, too. Reckon this will be one helluva claim.'

★ ★ ★

The following morning, I sat in the Ladies' Salon being waited on hand-and-foot by a very contrite landlord. Nothing was too much trouble. He'd rung Leeton Hospital to check on Sharon. They'd told him she had only a little smoke damage to her lungs plus scratches and would be released later that day. They'd checked out Doreen's asthma too.

I had bruises and cuts everywhere. I'd put on some slacks and a long-sleeved blouse after one of the longest showers I'd ever had. Even so, I stank of smoke — although it was probably from the hotel itself. Thankfully my possessions were mostly intact when Jimmy and his son moved them to a huge room at the front of the hotel.

After brekkie, Jimmy and I walked outside to survey the damage. It wasn't as bad as it seemed at three o'clock. Of the five rooms on the first floor facing the rail line, three had windows broken. Mine was the closest to the hole in the ground where the rail truck had once been. Metal debris and bits of the wheeled bogies were strewn around like dead leaves. It was a sobering sight.

The single-storey ex-bank extension would need rebuilding as it was unsuitable for living in. Those barred windows had almost killed young Sharon. I was amazed she'd survived.

Two firemen were shifting wreckage and putting salvageable furniture and possessions to one side. The pools of water from last night were evaporating from the ground, leaving cracked mud blotches. Occasionally the guys stopped to hose down a still-smouldering chunk of wood.

'I wanted to thank you for what you did, Amy,' Jimmy said gruffly. 'Wanted to apologise for yesterday too. The thought of losing another child . . . well, it makes you think.'

'You do realise that Doreen believes Graham is alive? Maybe you should, too. She needs that hope — she might not be as strong as you.'

I wondered if I was overstepping the boundary with this almost total stranger.

He laughed. 'Naw. My Doreen's strong all right. Always has been. Reckon you're right about supporting her more, though. You're pretty smart for a girlie teacher. Brave, too.' He rubbed a hand over his neck. 'Sorry, shouldn't call you a girlie. Bad habit. Gurawang's been let down by the bloke you're replacing. He cleared off without any notice just before school broke up mid-December.'

That explained my late appointment. Normally even a new teacher would have a month's notice. I had four days.

'Anyways, Amy, I figure I'd better tell you about our town. By the way, you're welcome to stay in our hotel as long as you want — free, of course. Least we can do. I know Doreen would agree. There's nowhere else to stay locally. Course, you could always do what the other young schoolies do — live in Leeton and drive in every day?'

I grinned. 'No car. I've a few days before school starts. Something might turn up. But thanks.'

'Fair enough. The offer's open. Betcha don't know where the name Gurawang comes from?'

I'd done a bit of research once I discovered where I was appointed.

'Aboriginal for a long-nosed bandicoot, right?'

Jimmy nodded, impressed.

'Wiradjuri tribe. A few families live hereabouts. Our town's been here since the 1850s. Captain Starlight was around these parts for awhile too. Sad to say, that's our biggest claim to fame.'

I'd heard of the infamous bushranger from an Aussie book I'd read in school; *Robbery Under Arms*. America's wild,

wild west had nothing on some of our outlaws.

We wandered back inside the relative cool of the hotel. I settled down on a seat in the lounge to sip a pub squash while Big Jimmy excused himself to make a phone call about the insurance. He wasn't looking forward to it.

He'd suggested that I ring home to let them know I was OK. 'No charge,' he'd said.

I decided against worrying Mum and Dad unnecessarily right now.

The icy drink tasted good. Sitting back in the comfy lounge, I considered the people I'd met so far. They all seemed genuinely decent once you cut through the tough dinki-di Aussie exterior of the men. Working out here in the outback bred a stronger, more down-to-earth type of people than I was used to from living in Sydney's suburbs.

I'd heard that country women were still treated as . . . not exactly second-class, but more as someone who was a wife or a mother. At a pinch, women were OK for teaching nursery and primary kids — however being a high school teacher like me would raise a few chauvinistic eyebrows.

I was so lost in thought, I didn't hear anyone enter the room behind me.

'Excuse me, Miss.' The gravelly voice made me jump. 'Amy Shaw? Come with me. Quickly.'

3

I twisted my head to see an elderly, balding man in khaki overalls and a checked shirt, limping towards me.

Talk about enigmatic, I thought. Despite him seeming harmless enough, I wasn't budging.

'I'm not going anywhere, mister. At least 'til you explain what this is all about.'

He appeared shocked by my refusal, glancing around furtively like a kid who'd been caught with his hand in the bikkie tin.

'Sorry. It's just that I shouldn't be here. I'm Mr Levinson . . . Cyril. My wife is waiting outside to talk to you.' He was becoming very agitated. His voice was shaking as he kept touching his glasses, nervously.

'What about?'

'You. You need somewhere to stay,

40

don't you? We have a room in town and can offer you board.'

Ah! I beamed at him. 'Lead on, Mr Levinson.'

In spite of his bad leg, he almost seemed to sprint from the pub. I had trouble keeping up.

We walked out into the harsh sunlight and down to a big old Ford Falcon, parked in the shade of the general store. Mr Levinson opened the back door for me before climbing in at the driver's side. He and, I presumed, Mrs Levinson, half-turned to face me.

'Our apologies for meeting out here, Miss Shaw,' the elderly woman said. 'Mr Levinson and me don't approve of alcohol or pubs. We're church-goers. That's why we asked you out here. We're retired farm folk and moved into town last year. Having heard about you wanting a place to stay, we'd ask you to consider boarding with us.'

She was in her late sixties, quite matronly with her long hair now mostly grey, neatly arranged in a bun. She was old-style Aussie, just like my gran. Even the heavy dark-rimmed glasses were similar. There was no make-up, not even lipstick and the lines on her tanned face told of a long, harsh life on the land. I was certain that she would expect younger people to call her by her surname.

Moreover, like Gran, she was in charge of the marriage now. Mr Levinson had probably spent his lifetime working with sheep and wheat. It had taken its toll on his body so he was happy to take it easy now. If Mrs Levinson wanted to offer me board at their home, he'd be fine with that.

'Would you like to take a look? It's not much but we like it. We're right next to Doctor MacAlister's house and surgery on the edge of town. It's walking distance to the school, too.'

I assumed they knew a lot about me already including my lack of transport; the joys of small towns and gossip. Out here if you didn't have a truck, a car or a ute you'd be totally up the creek.

'I'd love to. And please, call me Amy. We'll leave the Miss Shaw for my pupils, OK?'

'As you wish . . . Amy. Come on, Cyril. What are you waiting for?'

The six-cylinder engine spluttered to life. Cyril selected drive on the column and we moved off.

'This is the main street. You've seen the store. There's two banks, a bakery, butcher and two garages. Just here's the agricultural shop owned by a thieving pile of sheep droppings called Gilmore. None of us farmers like him much . . . just in case you hadn't guessed.'

'Mother! Language!' Mr Levinson must have been driving at five miles an hour, though there weren't any other cars in sight.

'Well, he is. Sheep droppings, I mean. My apologies for my language, Amy, but I says what I think. Always have. That's it for our main street. Unfortunately the nearest chemist is in Leeton but the store has most things. The school and churches are on the next street over along with our RSL club and tennis courts. They have floodlights if you like tennis. Turn here, Cyril.'

'I know the way, Mother.'

'Mr Levinson forgets things at times.'

Four hundred yards from the pub to the other end of the town, and only a few streets in depth. We crossed the rail line without Cyril checking. I hoped it was because he knew the timetable.

A right turn into Kookaburra Road revealed two brick houses, the first ones I'd seen. All the other homes were the usual Australian weatherboard with 'tin' roofs of corrugated iron.

'Ours is the second one,' Mrs Levinson informed me.

The house appeared quite large, having a well tended garden at the front with a veggie patch and wire-enclosed chicken coop at the rear.

Once inside, I was shown around. That included what would be my bedroom, which was lovely. The powder-blue walls seemed so fresh and the window looked out onto a flower bed, filled with Australian natives like bottlebrush and kangaroo paw with its distinctive red and green flowers. In addition there was a large scarlet waratah, the symbol of New South Wales. I hadn't seen one as beautiful before.

Elsewhere there was a second shower, sink and toilet in the laundry which was accessed from the kitchen/ dining room on one side and the double garage on the other. That would be for my use alone, an arrangement that suited me. I'd never boarded before and the thought of living in a stranger's house was scary. Nevertheless the rent they proposed of fifteen dollars a week was far less than I expected, and that included meals.

We sat in the kitchen, chatting over tea and pumpkin scones and agreed to 'see how it goes'. Mrs Levinson had concerns about having another boarder as the last young woman had proved quite a handful with her drinking and late nights. I assured her that I wasn't like that.

Mr Levinson drove me back to the hotel, where Jimmy brought my possessions out.

'Between you and me, you've got a good family there. Not exactly my sort, Amy, but they'll look after you,' he said in an undertone as we shook hands. His friends were collecting Doreen and Sharon from the hospital that afternoon. Both were apparently fine.

★ ★ ★

After unpacking back at Kookaburra Road, I helped Mrs L prepare lunch. She was soon talking to me as though we'd known each other for years. I suspected she'd long since run out of things to say to Mr L. Anyway, he was more than content to tend to the chooks and his veggie patch.

Having washed up and dried our plates, I was ready to sort out my room. Unlike my younger brother, I kept my bedroom back in Bondi tidy.

As the last fork was dried, the doorbell rang. I offered to get it as Mrs L clearly had problems walking quickly. It was probably some of their relatives, although there was no way I could recall who was who from the conversations over lunch; two daughters, a son plus five or six grandchildren.

'Who is it, dear?' Mrs L called out.

'The police,' I answered, surprised to see Kyle so soon.

'Well. Invite the Senior Constable in.'

'Sorry. Please come inside.'

'Just to say hi. I'd like you to accompany me back to the crime scene if that's OK.'

As he went to speak to Mr and Mrs L, I put on some comfortable shoes. I checked my dressing table mirror to make sure I was presentable. However with my short-sleeved blouse, my darkening bruises from last night were clearly visible. Great.

Nevertheless, it was too hot to change. On impulse I grabbed my straw hat and sunglasses.

Returning to the lounge room, I promised I'd be back before teatime, which was seven o'clock.

Following the Senior Constable to his car, I had a chance to weigh him up, at least from the back. Six foot one, probably fifteen stone, built like someone who could handle himself in a fight. However something in his demeanour suggested he was a negotiator rather than a brawler; maybe the confidence in his body language.

Seeing the holstered gun at his side, I was reminded that he was a no-nonsense copper, similar to the ones on the Aussie cop shows like *Division Four* or *Homicide*. His accent was more citified than the locals I'd met, indicating he'd grown up elsewhere. On reflection, having a local bloke as a copper might lead to all sorts of conflicts; arresting your own dad, for instance.

Kyle opened the passenger door. It

was a white two-door Monaro, a coupé that had been on the Aussie market for less than a year. All the young blokes wanted one. The four blue lamps were prominent on the roof.

'Five-litre?' I asked as he slid into his bucket seat beside me.

'Five point three. You know your cars, Amy?'

'My dad's a revhead. Actually drove in the Redex Trials back in the early fifties.'

That piqued his interest. The Redex Round Australia Trials were front-page news at the time. The long-distance endurance tests pushed both the cars and their drivers to the limits.

'Hold on. You're Amy Shaw. Your dad was Paul 'The Possum' Shaw, wasn't he? No wonder you're such a tough girl.'

'Actually I think I'm old enough to be a woman, Senior Constable,' I replied coolly.

'My apologies. I didn't mean to insult you. It's just that 'Possum' Shaw was my hero back then; the way he used to sneak past other drivers.'

'It's OK, I get a bit sensitive at times. I guess now I'm a teacher, I feel people should regard me differently even though I'm probably only four years older than some of the kids I'll be teaching. Anyway, better get a wriggle on before I melt.'

'Yeah. Definitely.' He set off to the far end of Gurawang. We could have walked. 'I wanted you to show me everything that happened at The Railway last night. Apparently that guy you saw broke into the reinforced truck on the siding. He stole most of a box of gelignite that was meant to blast a short cut further down the track. It looks like he left enough to destroy any evidence. Lit a fuse before scarpering.'

I turned in shock.

'You're telling me some lunatic left a van full of explosives on the edge of town? The whole place could have been destroyed.'

'Too right. My boss has already torn

the heads off a few railway employees. There'll be a lot of upset people when he and the local member are through. And some bloke is running around with enough jelly to blow up Warragamba Dam.'

I shuddered. What would anyone want with all that explosive? It was a sobering thought.

★ ★ ★

At the hotel, we wandered around inside and outside. I felt sick at what might have happened to Sharon and me. We'd been lucky.

Kyle took notes of all I told him. His questions were factual and incisive.

'What are you searching for?' I asked as he carefully examined the scattered metal fragments.

He stood up, a padlock in his gloved hand.

'They told me the truck was secure; heavy-duty lock plus the reinforced walls, roof and floors. The thief shouldn't have broken through it, even with cutters. Yet he did. What do you make of this?'

I took off my sunnies to peer at it. A whiff of Old Spice aftershave distracted me for a moment.

'Looks like it's been melted.'

'Must have been pretty damn hot to do that.'

I didn't answer right away. Instead I went over to something I'd spotted moments earlier. Picking it up, I returned to Kyle.

'Is that a sparkler?' he asked with interest.

'A dead one, yes. If you look at the lock there's a fine white powder on some parts. I think Mr Mystery has melted the lock using thermite. We studied it last year in chemistry at teaching college. Have you time for me to show you how it works? The science lab at the school should have the ingredients.'

'Yeah. I've found what I wanted and it's far too hot. Looks like I'll be your student for today.'

We called at the headmaster's house to pick up the key to the laboratory. The head, Colin, wasn't there but his wife, Judith, made us welcome. She expressed concern at my battered face and arms, giving me a tub of ointment.

Armed with the keys, we entered the room with attached store that would serve as my science lab while I taught at the central school. Due to the low number of students both in the town and on farms up to twenty miles away, the traditional school arrangement of Infants, Primary and High Schools had been combined to the more common country equivalent. Central schools taught all pupils from five to sixteen years old, although I would teach only high school students.

I unlocked the store room. Most of the bottled chemicals were arranged alphabetically on shelves within glass-fronted cupboards.

'What are you looking for, Amy? I can help.'

'Powdered aluminium, iron or ferric oxide and magnesium ribbon. I'll get the rest.'

I needed a container that would hold the mixture safely, plus a Bunsen burner. Having arranged them in the fume cupboard, I tried the Bunsen. No gas.

'Kyle,' I called. 'Do they have piped gas here?'

'You're joking, right? Propane or butane tanks.'

I explained the problem so he went out with the keys to turn the bottle gas on. In no time, I had the Bunsen alight on safety flame and had mixed the aluminium and iron oxide, placing a magnesium fuse in the mixture.

'You ready, Kyle? This is a thermite reaction. I reckon our thief used a sparkler to ignite the magnesium wick as he didn't have a Bunsen. Matches wouldn't burn hotly enough.'

I lit the fuse with the Bunsen and closed the safety glass sash window. The magnesium burst into a blinding light, similar to the flashbulbs where it was commonly used. Soon the mixture caught alight too, burning at a temperature around two thousand five hundred degrees Centigrade.

'Wow!' commented Kyle, feeling the heat from a yard away. 'That poor old lock wouldn't have stood a chance. That solves the how — yet who could know about this and have the materials?'

'Apart from brilliant, good-looking female science teachers, you mean?' I blushed, realising how stupid that must have sounded. 'Well . . . um, railway workers. They use thermite to melt tracks together. Also the Army, I guess.'

'The railway connection seems the most probable. I'll let my boss know what you've suggested. At least now we've got a clue who may have done it. Still don't know why, though.'

★   ★   ★

On the way back to the Monaro, I had a thought.

'Seeing as I was a consultant on this

case, does that mean I might get a fee for helping out?'

It was a cheeky suggestion but as Gran used to say, *If you don't ask, you don't get.*

'Pay? Doubt it. But I can invite you around to my place for a meal when you're settled in. Me and Tuesday would love to have you.'

'You and Tuesday?' At first I thought it was a strange name then I remembered Tuesday Weld, who'd been an American film star. I used to collect photos from the back of Fantale caramel choccie boxes; hers was one I had in my scrapbook.

Unfortunately it wasn't just the name that caught my attention.

'I thought . . . no, it didn't matter what I thought.'

He was just doing his job as a copper and it was dumb of me to read any more into the time we'd spent together today.

★   ★   ★

Tea was a simple salad affair with cold meats and Cheddar cheese. That suited me fine. I'd enjoyed helping Mrs L prepare it using a lot of fresh veggies and salad from the garden. Washing up also helped me relax and try to forget the past twenty-four hours with its highs and lows.

Quite frankly, I was looking forward to simply teaching, without explosions and fires and policemen who were married.

It was still a bright evening when I excused myself to go to my room. It had been made clear that I could join Mr and Mrs L watching telly. *Division Four* was on, one of my favourites, but I wasn't in the mood for police shows.

The setting sun was casting long rose-tinted shadows across the garden as I sat listening to the clucking chooks and the raucous laughter of a kook-aburra perched on a ghost gum just outside the fence.

'What have you got to be so blinking happy about, you stupid bird?' I muttered. 'You're not three hundred miles from home, missing everyone you love.' As for teaching properly for the first time, I was scared stupid despite my bravado. I would be the only science teacher there, relying on my intensive training in Sydney to get me by. Was I ready?

At least I was confident I'd have no discipline problems, despite my petite stature. I'd proved that in my practical teaching experience over twenty weeks while at college. All those six foot rugby-playing boys who believed I'd be a pushover, being a trainee teacher as well as a 'skinny sheila'? They were soon put in their places.

I wondered what my family would be doing now. Simple answer — watching *Division Four*. Of course the twins wouldn't, because it was a bit too violent for them. They'd be in their room with Frisky, our Siamese cat, lying on one of their beds while they played with their Barbies, discussing princesses or fairies.

I started to cry and despite dabbing my eyes with a clean hanky, the tears soon overwhelmed me as I broke into great heaving sobs. Nothing was right. I should be home where I belonged. Huge, exciting adventures in the middle of the Outback weren't for me. Not any longer.

I heard a discreet knock on my door.

'Are you all right, dear?'

It was Mrs Levinson. I stammered something.

'May I come in?'

What could I say? Part of me didn't want me to be seen in this state, though another part needed someone . . . anyone . . . to be there with me.

'Of course.'

Mrs L entered hesitantly. I dabbed my eyes again, thinking how terrible I must appear. At least my eyes would match my hair.

'May I sit with you a moment, sweetie?'

I nodded, looking down at the sodden handkerchief in my hands.

'You haven't had the best start to your stay in our town, Amy. For that I'm truly sorry.'

I stared at her face. There was genuine compassion there.

'It wasn't your fault. Why should you be sorry?'

'The people here try to look after the newcomers in our town, especially young ones like yourself. I understand it's a stressful time moving away from family the first time. It's not the same, but I remember how upset I was when Vince, our eldest, went to board at Yanco. He was twelve years old yet, to me, he was still my baby. I imagine it was much worse for him.'

'I . . . I really appreciate what you and Mr L are doing for me. Sorry, Mr Levinson.'

Mrs L smiled warmly and patted my hand.

'It's all right to call us Mr and Mrs L. As for having you board with us, I think it will be good for everyone. Mr L is showing more vitality than I've seen in ages. He misses the farm so much.'

'May I ask why you made me your offer?'

She put her hand on mine.

'Doreen told us what you did for her Sharon. Said you were like some sort of Supergirl, smashing that door down. We might not approve of what Doreen and Jimmy do with the hotel, but we respect her opinion. She told us you were a good 'un. So asking you to board here was the least we could do. I . . . I'm wondering if ringing your family might help you feel better.'

'I plan on speaking to them in the next few days from school.'

'Why wait? Give them our number. They can call any time it suits them. Besides, I wanted to have a quick word myself to reassure your mum. I know what it's like.'

I felt better already.

'By the way, it was Mr Levinson who suggested this. Don't tell him I told you so.' She sniffed the air. 'I think those clothes of yours could do with a good air, Amy. They smell of smoke. I'll hang them out on the line tomorrow.'

'I'll do that. I think it's not just my clothes, though. I had a shower this morning. I think I'll have another one, if that's OK.'

'You don't need to ask. You're part of this house now, young lady.'

'I just realised. You've been missing out on the telly. Sorry.'

She shook her head.

'Don't worry, Amy. I don't like police shows much. All that violence. Could I ask, though, sweetheart — are you too big for a hug?'

I grinned. 'I thought you'd never ask.'

⋆　⋆　⋆

Half an hour later, I was relishing the warm shower in the laundry. The screen door leading to the garage was locked and Mr L had already closed up outside for the night. Over the sound of the water I suddenly heard another noise of moving metal, followed by footsteps. I turned off the shower to peek around the screen door.

'The screen door's locked, Tracey. It's never locked. And the light's on.'

I reached out to grab my towel just as a face pressed up against the fly-screen netting.

Who was out there? Perhaps if I kept quiet they'd go away.

'Wait! I see someone. In the shower. It's a . . . '

'Get out. Now!' I yelled. Although it came out like a squeaky scream, it had the desired effect. A woman's face appeared at the door.

'Sorry. Didn't know Mum and Dad had company. We'll leave you. So sorry.'

The garage door slammed and I heard the lock engage. I never dressed so fast in my life.

Mum and Dad, they said. I wound the towel around my head before daring to go inside.

In the kitchen was a woman of about forty, dressed in jeans and a floral blouse.

'Apologies for the shock,' she said. 'My husband doesn't usually break in on women having showers. Amy, is it? Mum's just told us who you are. I'm Tracey, Vince's wife.'

Vince from Yanco. The eldest son. I reached out to shake Tracey's hand. She was pretty, and tanned from working on the land. We walked through to the lounge where a very apologetic Vince jumped to his feet.

'We always come in through the laundry, love. So sorry to shock you. Found this on the front doorstep and it's addressed to you.'

The plain envelope had my full name, in letters cut from some newspaper or magazine.

'I don't like the look of this,' I muttered, feeling a frisson of cold, in spite the warm evening. Handing it back, I stared at Vince.

'Can you please open it?'

I could see more glued-on letters on the page as he read it then showed it to the rest of us.

Mrs L gasped. 'Oh, my.'

Keep your moralizing nose to your-self or you'll end up like that Graham brat.

I staggered back in shock. The message was clear. One day in Gurawang and my life was already being threatened.

4

It was a good thing the doctor gave me something to help me sleep. Valerian, he called it; one of those natural herbs. As morning sunshine flooded my room, I woke and lay trying to make sense of it all.

Mrs L called me for brekkie at seven. I gave her a hand, chatting about nothing and everything; that is, everything apart from the note. She invited me to attend church with them and I accepted.

Although I'd been brought up C of E, I used to go to any religious class I'd fancied simply to learn a bit about other viewpoints. A few heads had turned when I'd gone to the Jewish class.

'We're Methodists. The Presbyterians use the same church on alternate weeks and we go then too. You'll like Reverend

Fletcher and his wife. After lunch, I thought you might fancy going out to our old farm. Vince and Tracey run it now.'

'How big is it?'

'Just over ten thousand acres. Not that big.'

To a city girl like me, ten thousand acres sounded pretty darn large.

'Yes. I'd love to come. If you're positive they wouldn't mind?'

Mr L opened the screen door to the back, clutching a small pail with eggs in it. He kicked his boots off on the mat. As he did so, a sheet of paper blew down from the old dresser in the kitchen. It was the letter from last night.

'Sorry, dear. I did mean to pop it in a drawer. Out of sight . . . '

'I was wondering about fingerprints,' Mr L suggested.

'So was I,' I said, pleased that Mr L was involved. 'However, apart from all of us handling it, I somehow don't reckon the bomber would be that much of a drongo. The letter does tell us all one thing, though.'

'What's that, Amy?'

'That Graham didn't get lost. He was taken. I'm praying that somewhere he's still alive.'

'Taken? But why?' said Mr L.

'Can't work that out . . . yet.'

Mrs L was on her feet heading for the phone.

'What are you doing?' I inquired.

'Asking the Senior Constable to call around.'

'I'll tell him over the phone. Today is Sunday and I'd like it to be as normal as possible. At least for the moment. Please?'

'You and Kyle had a falling-out, Amy? Sorry. None of my business.' Mr L stirred his mug of tea, before easing himself onto a chair. He removed his glasses to rub his eyes.

'No, we haven't. And you don't need to apologise. It's simply I don't want the bomber to have any more information about me and what I'm doing.

68

That threat last night was due to me being seen with Kyle. The bomber must be watching me. He clearly knows I'm living here 'cause he placed the envelope on your doorstep. No, it's best if I do normal things. Let the bas . . . sorry, bathtub, believe that he's scared me off.'

'Actually you can say 'bastard', Amy. That's what he is. He blew up that wagon, almost killing sweet little Sharon. And from what you say, Graham's missing because of him,' Mrs L reassured me.

'Not broadcasting her suspicions to everyone? It makes sense, you know, Mother.'

'Exactly. Told you she was clever, Father. We should all behave normal-like. Like he's frightened us off investigating. Who wants what for breakfast?'

'Don't suppose you have any Sugar Frosties? They're my favourite,' I piped up.

Mr L's weathered face broke into a broad grin.

'My favourite too. *Shot full of sugar.*' It was the catchphrase used on the telly ads.

As Mrs Levinson brought the cereal packet to the table, we stared at the front with its photo of Smoky Dawson, Australia's own singing cowboy.

'I met him once. Even rode his horse, Flash,' I told them. 'I was twelve at the time.'

The intimidating letter was forgotten again, by everyone bar me. How would Smoky deal with young Graham's kidnappers? I mused. Ride in with six guns blazing? That wouldn't work in real life. Out here, things had to be done more surreptitiously. And, threats or no threats, I was going to do my best to solve the mystery.

★   ★   ★

Mrs L was right about the Reverend and his wife, Barbara. She was bubbly, friendly and interested in everything about me. Talk about welcoming.

Barbara was about thirty, younger than Reverend Fletcher. She made a point of introducing me to the others in the congregation. All those new names were a lot for me to take in. It was easier for them, of course. They were all friends. In fact, half were probably related in one way or another. Frank's comments about the gene pool sprang to mind; there were definite family resemblances.

Barbara took the children off to the annex for Sunday School. It was amusing to watch the kiddies' expressions. *Our new teacher*, they must have been thinking as they filed off, staring at me as though I was a strange animal in a zoo.

The majority would be younger than my pupils yet they'd see me every day around the school. I couldn't imagine the dynamics of a central school; mature teenagers playing marbles or chasies with five-year olds, It seemed . . . well, bizarre.

Vince and Tracey were there, along

with one of Mr and Mrs L's daughters. I spent the sermon trying to put names to the faces of people seated by me as I listened to the Reverend.

Afterwards, one of the ladies commented on the length of my dress. It was hardly a mini, ending slightly above my knee. I could sense there'd be a bit of getting used to out here as far as differing attitudes went.

Was one of the men here the bomber from last night? All I knew was that he had a moustache. Regrettably, it was 1970. Half the men in Oz had a moustache and, glancing around, that fashion had definitely reached Gurawang, even if the length of ladies' dresses hadn't. He could have been any of half a dozen blokes here.

I'd have to choose my confidants carefully. If I spoke to the wrong person about my investigation, then I understood that the bomber could make my life difficult.

I was more concerned about Mr and

Mrs L. The last thing I wanted was for them to be under peril of injury . . . or worse.

* * *

Returning home for lunch, I assisted Mr L with picking fresh veggies for our salad. I was amazed at what he grew. Fresh salad was so much better than the daggy stuff in the greengrocers in Bondi.

While I buttered bread to eat with lunch, I broached the subject. 'Maybe it would be better if I moved elsewhere. There's no way I want you two involved in the danger to my life.'

Mrs L put her knife and fork down, reaching across to grasp my hands.

'Nonsense, Amy. We're here to support you, through thick or thin. In any case, we're as involved as you. All of us are. Graham — the missing boy? He's a relative of ours. Doreen's our niece.'

Mr L joined in. 'What you said this

morning, about him being kidnapped. In spite of it sounding terrible, it's given Mother and me optimism. He could still be alive. Wandering off and getting lost, we figured he'd be surely dead. But if he was taken away, there's a good chance the youngster's still alive.' He put his large hand on ours. 'That hope you've given us. It's so important.'

'I'll give the police a ring about the note and my suspicions after lunch,' I told them, reassured. 'We'll find out the connection between Graham and the bomber bloke . . . '

'Can't we come up with a better name than 'bomber bloke'?' Mrs L asked.

Mr L grinned, his eyes suddenly sparkling.

'Moriarty. The villain from — '

'*Sherlock Holmes*. That's brilliant, Mr L.' I cut a tomato and held one piece in front of my mouth, pretending it was my new-found nemesis. 'Whoever you are, Mr Moriarty, your days are numbered.' Crunching on that poor defenceless tomato was so satisfying.

Mrs L gave me the number for the local police station. I half expected that Tuesday might answer. As luck would have it, she didn't.

'Police. How can I help?' His deep voice reminded me of our eventful meetings.

'Kyle. It's me, Amy Shaw. There's been a development.' I explained about the note.

He wanted to come around immediately until I told him my reasons for keeping things low-key. Once I read the intimidating note, he came to the same conclusion that I'd already reached.

'Some bloke's snatched Graham. That explains why we couldn't find any trace of him. We considered it, but there was no ransom demand. Plus Jimmy and Doreen are hardly rolling in money. No, this puts a whole new complexion on the situation. I do need to see that note, Amy.'

I repeated my concerns. 'I don't want

to be seen with you.' I heard a sound of surprise at my flat statement. 'We're out this arvo anyway.'

'Where? Where you off to?' His voice was slightly too brusque for me. Copper-mode.

'Out to Vince and Tracey's. Not that it's any of your business, Senior Constable.'

'Then I'll see you there. I'll take a different road. I hardly think this bomber-guy will follow either of us. That way we'll keep our meeting under the radar. He won't suspect anything.'

'He's called Moriarty. The bomber-guy, I mean.'

'Weird name. Do you think he's a foreigner? Should I put out an All Points Bulletin?'

I giggled before explaining the reason Mr L and I had decided on the code-name. Seemed like not everyone was aware of Sir Arthur Conan Doyle's detective and his arch adversary.

The tension was broken. We agreed on a time.

'Do bring the envelope too, Miss Shaw.' His overly polite tone was now tongue-in-cheek.

'Oh my goodness. The envelope! Where is it?' Had I tossed it in the bin? I tried to remember.

Mr L, who'd been listening along with his wife, produced a paper bag with the item inside.

'Evidence,' he explained with a smug nod.

'It's OK, we have that as well. Mr L would make a great detective. He'd already bagged it.'

'See you soon, Amy.'

'Yeah. See you soon . . . Kyle.'

★ ★ ★

At one o'clock, we all set off in the Falcon to visit the Levinsons' former farm. What surprised me was that they suggested I should drive.

'Mr Levinson don't see so good in the dark, so if you could drive back tonight we could stay out there awhiles longer. Seems only fair to find out how you go, driving in the daylight first.'

'I've never driven an automatic before,' I protested.

Mr L stepped in. 'No worries, Amy. It's the same as a manual, only different. No clutch. Just point it where you want to go. You do have a licence, don't you?'

'Oh yes. And I don't need P plates any more.'

I looked the console over. It was pretty well the same as my dad's two-year-old Holden, except much older and humungously bigger. The odometer read over two hundred thousand miles. Country driving, I guessed.

'OK, if you're comfortable with that. I'll need a cushion for the seat, though.'

Or maybe a ladder, I thought. The dash was high and, automatic or not, I needed to see where I was going.

I turned the ignition on once we were

seated. Mrs L was in the back, behind me.

'You can only start it in P or N. R's for Reverse and D's for Drive.'

'There doesn't seem to be any petrol.'

'The gauge is broke. I always keep her topped up, though. Did it yesterday,' Mr L said quietly.

Mrs L spoke up. 'I heard that, Father. You promised to get it fixed last week.'

Mr L turned his head. 'Well I forgot, didn't I?'

'Silly old galah. You'll forget your own name one of these days.'

'Which way?' I selected Drive.

'Left, then second right, Amy. And Mother, I do know my own name. It's . . . it's . . . Horace.'

He gave me a wink.

'No, it's not! Horace was your first horse,' Mrs L exploded. Then I saw her grin as she realised. 'All right. Have your fun, Cyril Levinson. Or should I really call you Horace? Just to teach you a lesson.'

'Neighhh,' Mr L replied. We all laughed.

Then I remembered that this fun interlude wasn't reality; a disappearing child and explosions were. What would Kyle make of the written threat and would it help us find the man I called Moriarty?

★   ★   ★

We were out of town before I realised it, driving along a road that simply stretched into the distance before us. Talk about straight. There were no hills or mountains, only shades of ochre as far as we could see. Occasionally a clump of straggly gum trees would break the monotony.

In school, we were taught a poem by Dorothea MacKellar. *I love a sunburnt country, a land of sweeping plains . . .* Two out of every three years were droughts in Australia. Lush green paddocks did not happen. And yet, the harsh Aussie countryside certainly had its own beauty.

'How far to your old farm?' I asked.

A flight of sulphur-crested cockatoos swooped overhead. We could hear their raucous screams.

'Twenty-three miles from town,' Mr L replied.

'What's that in kilometres?'

'Around thirty-five.' Australia was altering all measurements to metric in a year or so.

'Bad enough they had to change from pounds, shillings and pence back in sixty-six. Those funny dollar notes still seem like the money in Monopoly. I don't think I'll ever learn this metric stuff, though. It's too hard on the older people. Too confusing,' Mrs L commented behind me.

It was true. A man on the moon, a new Opera House being built on the harbour, even talk of colour telly. Australia was changing; growing up, some were saying.

'Over there.' Mr L pointed, momentarily blocking my vision. 'That's where Graham disappeared. The creek runs through them trees.'

I took my eyes from the Tarmac for an instant. This was the only road nearby so if he was grabbed, they must have parked here and snuck up on him by foot.

'If he was overpowered then brought back to the car, how could someone hold him while driving off?' I speculated as we continued past.

'Knock him out? Use . . . oh, what do they call it? Chloroform?' Mr L suggested.

'Bundle him in the boot? No, he'd make such a racket his mates would have heard,' Mrs L added, disappointed her idea didn't make sense.

'Or if there were two kidnappers?' I offered.

'Certainly worth mentioning to Kyle.' Mrs L gave a satisfied smile. I could see her in the rear vision mirror and suspected she was keen on some close relationship between us. Didn't she know he was married? Or, more likely, she didn't approve of Tuesday. Yeah, country life was going to take some getting used to — starting with me spending my Sundays hundreds of miles from the beaches instead of riding my surf board on the Sydney waves. Like that song by Spanky and Our Gang, my Sundays would never be the same.

★　★　★

Once we reached the farm itself Mr L announced, 'Welcome to Currawong Station.'

I gazed around the houses and outbuildings. It didn't seem as large as I'd thought.

'How many people work here?' I enquired.

'Just our son Vince, our grandson and Joe.'

I was surprised. We'd been driving for a while after Mr L announced we were driving alongside their old farm.

As we pulled up, Vince and his son Steven came over to us. Stephen had just left school and was even taller than his father, with long, lanky hair styled after modern pop groups.

They greeted us warmly. I felt blessed to be with such lovely people.

'Hi. You must be Steven,' I said, extending my hand. He looked away before taking it, shifting uncomfortably on his feet.

'Must be great working here on the farm?'

'Yeah. I guess. Can I go now, Dad? The top forty needs the fences checking.'

After he left, Mrs L had a quiet word with me.

'Don't take it personal, Amy. Steven's always been shy, especially around females. But he loves farm work.'

Vince spoke up. 'Why don't you head over to the sheds, Amy? Say hello to Joe. He's working on a tractor. I'll take Mum inside. Kyle can meet us out there. I'd prefer that Lucy didn't hear what we talk about. She and Graham were real close.'

I recalled that Lucy was Vince and Tracey's young daughter.

'I'll come with you, Amy,' said Mr L, almost stumbling over a bucket. I steadied him.

'Darn glasses. Eyesight's not that good these days. The joys of getting old.'

The shed or barn or whatever was massive. There were rotary hoes and other farm stuff neatly arranged. I'd seen pictures of the machinery in books, but never in real life. There wasn't much need for a combine harvester in Bondi.

We spied a bloke working on a huge tractor and headed over to him. He had his back turned, still wearing his broad-brimmed hat.

'How's it going, Joe? Like you to meet our new schoolie, Amy,' Mr L called out.

The man put down his spanner. When he faced me, I had a bit of a shock.

'You're an aboriginal?'

He examined his hands, turning them over.

'Gee. I guess I am.' Then he broke into the biggest smile I'd ever seen, his brilliant white teeth contrasting with his dark skin.

'And you speak English?'

'Amy, is it? I'm guessing you've never met an aboriginal before.'

Despite the cool shade, I felt my skin burning. I was being so rude.

'I'm . . . I'm so sorry. I didn't mean . . . To answer your question, no, I haven't.'

I'd met Italians, lots of Greeks, some Poms, a Ukrainian and a Celonese. My best friend in primary was Chinese. I thought I'd always been easy-going with other nationalities yet, right now, I felt so ashamed of my prejudice.

'Joe. I admit I was out of order. I don't know any aboriginals but my behaviour just now was terrible. I apologise. Can we start again?' I held out my hand. 'I'm Amy. Pleased to meet you.'

Without hesitation, he took off his work gloves to grasp my hand in his. They were huge.

'Pleased to meet you, Amy.'

Mr L spoke up. 'Joe's parents worked for me for years till they passed. Joe grew up with Vince. Saved his life more than once.'

It was obvious Cyril and Joe had a close bond.

'So what are you doing, Joe?' I asked. 'Tractor problems?'

'Yeah. Running rough when you start 'er up. Loss of power too. Can't figure it out.'

'Turn the ignition on. I might be able to help.'

Both men stared at me sceptically. I nodded towards the big beast of a machine.

'I might know nothing about tractors, yet I do understand engines.'

Joe fired her up and after twenty seconds, I signalled him to turn it off.

'Spark plugs are carbonised. Gaps too wide.'

I was referring to the gap where the petrol was ignited to provide the power.

'But they're new. Well, pretty new. Just had a service. I'll check, but reckon you're way off base, Miss.'

Within seconds he'd taken one out. The black carbon was clearly evident caking up the metal.

'Well I'll be. Cyril, she was dead right. Thanks for that, Amy. Thanks a lot.'

'You'll need to reset the gap. I can do it if you want.'

'Naw. I can do it. Don't dirty your pretty frock. Still can't believe a woman knowing 'bout motors.'

'I guess we all have our misconceptions, Joe.'

He grinned back at me.

'Yeah, Amy. Reckon you're right about that.'

Vince came in with Kyle following him.

'Cyril, Joe,' he said, shaking hands.

'I'll finish off later, Vince.' Joe made to leave.

'No — I think you should hear this, Joe. You spent days trying to find Graham.'

Cyril explained for my benefit.

'Joe's a tracker. Best in these parts. Can find anything that moves.' He addressed Joe. 'Seems young Graham was kidnapped.'

Joe seemed astounded. 'Kidnapped? Well, I'll be. That explains why I couldn't find the lad.'

Everyone read the letter after which Kyle took charge. 'So what does this tell us, fellas . . . and girl — sorry, woman?'

''Fellas' is fine, Kyle.' I smiled at his apparent unease. It was like a scene from one of my mystery crime novels; police gathering around Miss Marple to discuss clues. In this case the group consisted of Kyle, the copper, Vince and Cyril, farmers, Joe, the tracker and me, a younger Miss Marple. What a combination.

Vince spoke first. 'Stuck-down letters from some magazine? Wants to hide his handwriting so he's probably someone local.'

'He hand-delivered it, indicating he knew Amy had moved in with us. That backs up the local bit.' Cyril stared sadly at us all. 'I . . . I find that hard to believe. We're such a close-knit community.'

I said my bit next.

'Moriarty snatched Graham . . . '

'Moriarty?'

'It's what Amy and me call the bomber-guy.'

'Sherlock Holmes,' Joe told the others. 'Moriarty was the chief baddie. Go on, Amy.'

'We figured Moriarty took Graham from under the noses of Graham's mates at the creek, so he either knocked him out before driving off or . . . '

'There were two kidnappers,' Cyril explained.

'Kyle. Remember that cloth on the road near the creek? The one with the funny smell?' Joe was recalling the early hours of the search.

'Oh yeah. I do now. I put it in an evidence bag. It's in the boot still. I'll get it.'

While he was gone we checked the note again.

Keep your moralizing nose to yourself or you'll end up like that Graham brat.

'So what do the words tell us?' I asked.

'Well. This Moriarty doesn't like Graham so hopefully the boy's still alive and giving the criminal a hard time.' We nodded in unison. I felt that together, we were making progress. It was a good feeling. I'd never met Graham but I wanted to help find him more than anything; for Doreen and Jimmy, but strangely it was mostly for me.

Kyle returned, clutching a bag with the cloth. We took turns sniffing it. None of the guys recognised the odour but I did. I recalled Frank taking too long a sniff of the chemical at teaching college, passing out, dropping like a sack of spuds.

'Chloroform . . . they used chloroform to knock little Graham out. He didn't stand a chance.'

Joe broke the reflective silence.

'Well, he's not that bright. See how he spelled 'moralizing'. It should be with an 's' not a 'z'.'

I'd missed that.

Cyril had the answer. 'He's a Yank. This Moriarty low-life is American. I worked with them in the war. They have some funny ways of spelling.'

That prompted Kyle to add more info.

'There's a Yank working on the railways at Kirindoo Creek. Think he rents a place in town.'

Only a railway worker would know there was gelignite in that freight wagon.

'Seems like you need to question this bloke, Senior Constable.'

Kyle's face was grimly determined.

'Yeah, Amy. Reckon him and me are going to have an extremely lengthy discussion.'

★ ★ ★

It was nine o'clock when we left Currawong Station. Kyle had driven off before tea, as he had things to do. The barbecue had been fab.

I was a bit worried driving in the dark on a road I hardly knew. There were no street lights. The January night sky was pitch-black. The moon hadn't risen yet.

'How do I put the high beam on?' I asked. I'd never needed high beam driving around the suburbs of Sydney.

'There's a switch on the floor, Amy. You turn it on and off with your feet.'

I tried it and was amazed at how bright everything suddenly became.

'Just make sure that you turn it off when another car is coming.'

I doubted we would see another car. The expression 'middle of nowhere' came to mind.

We'd driven about five miles when the car gradually developed a splutter before conking out completely. The head and dashboard lights were on so I figured it wasn't electrical.

'What is it?' Mrs L asked. 'What's the problem?'

'Sounds like we're out of fuel,' I suggested.

'That's impossible,' Mr L said. I remembered that he'd recently filled it up.

'Easy enough to check,' I replied. 'Have you got a torch?' It happened that I'd parked us on the side of the road. We opened the boot and I crouched to examine the petrol tank. Perhaps a stone had caused a puncture. It was too difficult to see properly, so I decided I'd need to crawl underneath.

Mrs Levinson was standing by our side.

'What are you doing, Amy? You'll ruin that pretty frock of yours.'

'I haven't got much choice, I'm afraid.'

Mrs L rummaged in the boot.

'Here. Put this blanket down. And you'd better take that dress off.'

Mr L appeared quite uncomfortable.

'Don't worry, Amy. Mr L won't peek. Cyril, turn around and close those eyes of yours till I tell you to open them. Or bad things will happen.' She whispered, 'Probably can't see nothing, anyway.'

Trusting to Mrs L's eagle-eyed supervision, I carefully stepped from my dress, leaving my petticoat and bra on. Lying on the blanket I scrunched under the boot to shine the torch on the petrol tank.

No wonder we'd run out of fuel. A nail had been knocked into the tank, giving us a slow leak.

'Your car's been sabotaged,' I called out. 'We're stuck out here . . . at least for the night.' Moriarty was playing mind-games, leaving us stranded, miles from any houses. I was concerned about the Levinsons. They took medication around this time last night and hadn't brought any tablets with them.

I braced my hands to push me back out from under the car, only to feel movement under my left palm. It was difficult to twist my head and impossible to lift my head because of the car. My heart went into overdrive as I imagined what it might be. It felt cold and scaly, exactly like a . . .

'Mrs L? Are . . . are you there?' I called out in panic, not daring to budge. I could sense the thing coming closer so, ever so slowly, I tipped my head to the side.

'What is it, sweetheart?'

Two beady eyes examined me from less than two feet away as a forked tongue flicked the night air. My mouth went dry as my heart rate doubled. *Whatever you do*, I told myself, *don't panic.*

'I . . . I think I'm touching a big snake.'

5

I heard Mrs L shuffling around, I supposed to try and see. It would be a problem for her because I was the one with the torch, which was illuminating the car chassis and the surrounding gravel road.

I tried to nudge it so that she might have a better view of the creature.

'A snake? No, I don't think so, Amy. Actually, I think it's Marilyn. Let me . . . Yes, I can see the cut on her tail.'

The creature's terrifying face was edging closer to me. *So what on earth is a Marilyn?* I asked myself, perspiring like mad.

'Marilyn's a goanna — a giant lizard.'

'And . . . do goannas bite?' I had visions of dying from goanna poisoning.

'Not unless you're a little mousie or a frog. She's just curious.' Mrs L shuffled some more. 'Come here, Marilyn. Come to Mummy.'

When the creature turned away from me, I took a deep breath. Quickly, I wriggled out from under the car. The torchlight gave everything it touched an unreal appearance. Mrs L was bending down to stroke a five-foot-long lizard.

The reptile appeared very contented. I speculated that her guttural sounds were the lizard equivalent of a purr.

'That's Marilyn?'

'Yes. She used to live at Currawong. Once we left, she disappeared. We thought we'd lost her.'

'So why has she turned up here and now?'

'Dunno. I can only guess that she somehow recognised our car. She's normally getting her beauty sleep at night.' Mrs L turned towards her hubby then raised her voice. 'Father, it's Marilyn. She's here. Gave Amy a nasty fright, didn't you, you naughty thing!'

'So I can open my eyes now?'

'I suppose. But make sure you only

look at the ground in front of you
. . . or else.'

'G'day, Marilyn. How ya going?'

Mrs L turned towards me.

'Marilyn's a sand goanna. She used
to follow Mr Levinson everywhere.
Guess you could say she was like a pet.'

I gazed down at the huge lizard.
Some pet! Without altering the direction of his stare, Mr L asked if there
were a hole in the petrol tank.

'Yeah. I can repair it, at least to get us
home. Trouble is, we don't have any
petrol.'

'Not a problem, Amy. There's a spare
can in the boot. I used to be a Boy
Scout many years ago. *Be Prepared.*
That was our motto.'

'Pity you didn't remember that when
it came to fixing the blinking fuel
gauge, Father,' Mrs L reminded him.

He acknowledged defeat with a sigh.

'Right. You can close your eyes again
now.'

I took the torch to retrieve my
handbag.

'Don't tell me you have your repair kit in there?' Mrs L sounded intrigued.

'No. I do have the next best thing, though.'

There was an open packet of Juicy Fruit chewing gum inside a zippered compartment. The next few minutes must have been quite a sight. Mr L standing with his eyes closed like some statue, Mrs L stroking this giant lizard under its throat and me, wearing nothing except a petticoat, bra and shoes chewing madly on the gum. Maybe I should have brought my Polaroid? Then again, with me in my whitey-whites, maybe not.

The temporary repair was completed almost as fast as you could say Bullamakanka. After adding the petrol, we were soon on our way again.

There was an emotional farewell between the Levinsons and Marilyn. I'd never said goodbye to a reptile before, but she closed her eyes and — I swear — smiled as I also gave her a scratch.

'It was a good thing you were there,

Amy. We'd have been stranded all night, otherwise.'

I wasn't so sure. After all, me living with the Levinsons was the reason that Moriarty had punctured their petrol tank.

★　★　★

The following day was Australia Day, 1970. Two hundred years since Captain Cook had arrived — and only seventy years since Australia had become a proper country, instead of a group of neighbouring states.

After brekkie, we sat down in front of the telly to watch the celebrations happening in Sydney and the other capital cities. It was emotional for me since the last five years I'd been down at Sydney around Circular Quay to see the celebrations first-hand. They showed the partially built Opera house and the Harbour Bridge as well as the ferries I used to travel on so often. Even now, the Opera House was spectacular.

It would probably be another year before it was finished.

The feeling of national pride was tempered by the chat I had with Joe. When I'd mentioned the holiday, he'd put me in my place.

'Not special for me, Amy. Us aboriginals have been here for forty thousand years. For the last two hundred years we've been the ones treated like foreigners. You so-called Aussies only agreed to call us *people* three years ago. Before that, legally we didn't exist.'

It was a massive surprise to me. I should have known about it, yet I didn't. I felt ashamed and resolved to ask Joe a lot more questions. Somehow my knowledge of Aussie history that I'd been so proud of, felt suddenly tainted.

Because it was the last day before school started, I decided to do some preparation. I walked down Kookaburra Road to the school, hoping somebody would be there who could help me find out what I was supposed to be doing.

As I strolled along the veranda in front of the high school classrooms, an older guy in shorts and a T-shirt came from an office to ask what I was doing there. T-shirts weren't the best choice for a bloke with a beer-belly although he was far from the worst I'd seen; at least he wasn't displaying his belly-button for the world to see.

'Name's Amy Shaw. The new science teacher. Who are you?'

'Colin Anderson. I'm the headmaster. You met my wife the other day. Welcome to the school. If you have a few minutes, I'd like to discuss your classes with you. You can come to my office, if that's all right.'

'That's great. Thanks very much.'

I took off my hat as I sat at his desk, opposite him. The room seemed well organised. Obviously he enjoyed being on top of things.

'Those bruises look nasty, Amy. I heard about what you did the other night. That was very brave.'

I'd expected the contusions would be less noticeable. Sadly there were some parts of me that were the same blue as the Aussie flag. Not much I could do, apart from cover them up.

'You're the only new teacher here this year. You'll be teaching science, art, health and sport.'

'Wow. That sounds a lot. My training's for science alone . . . but I guess you're aware of that.'

'Out here, we have to do a bit of everything. There are only seventy pupils in the high school part. Three classes for the basic subjects; first year, second year, three and four are combined. I hope I'm not being too rude, when I say that you are extremely young. Twenty-one?'

'Twenty, actually. I've completed two years at teaching college. The education department set up a special course to train new science teachers because of the shortage throughout the state. It's called fast-tracking, apparently.'

'Twenty. And you don't have a degree? It's just frustrating from my point of view. They keep sending the inexperienced baby teachers out to the country.'

I bristled a bit. This was not going very well.

'Perhaps if more experienced teachers were willing to come, they wouldn't make it a condition of employment for new teachers to spend three years in the country. It's hardly my fault, Colin. I never heard of this place until a few days ago.'

He seemed about to raise his voice in defence then thought better of it.

'No, you're right. It's not your fault. We'll simply have to make the best of it, working together.' He relaxed into a wide grin. 'You have a quite a temper on you, don't you, Amy? Ready to speak your mind? That's good. Most of the other staff have been here so long, I believe some new blood might stir things up. Nothing wrong with that. How do you fancy a cuppa? And some Iced Vo-Vos?'

A peace offering with bikkies thrown in?

'Lead on, boss.'

We went together to the compact staff kitchen next to the high school staffroom. After the refreshments we both cleared up.

'Do you have a timetable for me?' I asked. 'I'd like to do some prep for tomorrow. I'm really looking forward to it.'

'I'll show you around, then I'll talk you through tomorrow's arrangements. It's not a big school, however the staff and the pupils are great. You'll enjoy it. I've been here two years myself, and I've loved every day of it. Well, almost. Unfortunately we had a situation with your predecessor. He caused a lot of problems in leaving when he did. And while I'm aware that you are very young to be a teacher, I've been very impressed from reading the reports of your practice teaching and your results in exams. I notice you failed the medical first time around. A dodgy knee?'

'It's usually not a problem. Synovial fluid. Water-on-the-knee. Gets swollen if I knock it. A bit painful but I take aspirin if I need to. Just happened to be playing up the day of the medical exam. I'm being reassessed in May so I'm expecting to pass then.'

Forty minutes later, I felt much more comfortable being in Gurawang. Colin reminded me so much of a tubbier Mr Brady out of *The Brady Bunch* even though his moustache looked more like a caterpillar on his top lip. Facial hair suited some people, but not everyone.

It was a shame that moustaches were all the rage for men these days. I preferred my boyfriends without furry faces. Not that I was in any hurry to fall in love — but a girl, even a copper-top like me, could still dream.

At the end of the tour, he apologised for making me take the art classes.

'There simply isn't anyone else.'

'It's fine. I do a lot of drawing in my

spare time so I'm sure I can do a fine job with the girls.'

The classes were split into males and females for the non-core subjects with the boys doing metalwork and woodwork while the girls did art and needlework. It seemed a bit unfair, as I would have loved to do the 'boy' subjects myself.

Parting ways at his office door, Colin inquired what I was doing that night. 'There's a dance in the village hall,' he explained.

'Hold on, Colin. Let me get this right. You're asking me to go to a dance with you?'

He broke into a deep laugh.

'Me? No way. Got two left feet. It was my wife's idea. She thought you might like to go with her. Nothing special, it's an excuse for a get-together for the town — they catch up on the news while having a bit of fun doing old-fashioned dances. None of the modern stuff like the Stomp, though.'

It seemed my new boss was a bit

old-fashioned himself. The Stomp hadn't been around for years.

'I used to be champion barn dancer in school,' I told him proudly. The Barn Dance, Pride of Erin, Gypsy Tap; I learned them in primary, dancing with guys from the boys' school. The cold, clammy hands of some had put me off boys for years.

'Sounds like you'll be right at home.'

'Better get back to my own preparation. One thing, though. Did you know that boy who disappeared very well?'

'I never taught him because he was in primary. Used to see him on class visits and in the playground. He was always joking with everyone as he had a lot of friends. Sorry, meant to say 'has'. We're still praying he will turn up yet, after all this time, I somehow doubt it.'

I decided not to inform him about our suspicions. At least, not until there was more evidence. Kyle had decided to speak to Doreen and Jimmy yesterday, to keep them informed. Finding the chloroform-soaked hankie was encouraging us all to believe that he was still alive.

I went to my lab. There were four science lessons tomorrow and two art. On impulse, I decided to check the chloroform in the prep room. The dark glass bottle was almost full. I felt relieved. At least it hadn't been taken from there.

★ ★ ★

That evening I caught up with Colin's wife, Judith, outside the village hall. Even though the sun had set, the western skies were still washed in an indigo blue. There seemed to be flocks of birds darting through the air above our heads.

Judith corrected my misconception.

'Actually they're bats. Fruit bats. We're not that far from the fruit trees in the irrigation area.'

We paid for our tickets at the door. The muted sounds of music filtered into the night air.

Once inside the hall, I felt everyone was staring at me. Judith squeezed my arm reassuringly.

'Don't worry, Amy. Most are having a stickybeak. You are kinda famous after the explosion.'

The hall was festooned with coloured lights and dozens of Aussie flags. Strangely, I noticed one or two New Zealand ones scattered among them.

When I pointed it out to Judith she responded, 'Out here, people aren't that particular. Close enough is good enough. By the way, Colin was quite impressed with you. Between you and me, he says that most of the other staff just coast along from year to year. The Living Dead, he calls them. You won't tell them, will you?'

It was a strange thing to divulge to a total stranger although I supposed Judith could see a kindred spirit in me, despite us only having just met. Some time in the past, she'd probably come from the Big Smoke and now felt trapped. Colin told me she was a trained nurse with nowhere to work. They didn't have children themselves. Apart from a few hours each day being the school's secretary she had too much time on her hands.

In addition, I could tell she'd been drinking. Perhaps her willingness to share confidences had more than a little to do with that.

She was in her mid-forties with long blonde hair, and very attractive. Once again, I found myself being introduced to total strangers, struggling to keep up with Judith's rapid-fire commentary about their jobs, their children and where they lived. She was like a whirlwind. Nevertheless, I suspected her apparent friendship with these people was pretence for my benefit. In spite of living in the community for two years, she wasn't a part of it. Exactly like me, she was passing through.

'And this is Beryl and Dick Norman. Lovely couple. Beryl runs the milk-bar, don't you, Beryl? And ... and Dick ... oh, I feel a bit giddy. Will you excuse me? I need to step out for a spot of air.'

'Do you want me to come with you, Judith?'

'Oh no, kiddo. I'll be right. You stay here and mingle. I'll just be a mo.'

Judith did seem a little pale. I decided to follow her, stopping once I saw her head off to a corner, to lift a metal flask from her bag. There was no alcohol allowed at this dance so, I supposed, Judith had brought her own.

Returning to Mr and Mrs Milk-Bar, I listened as Beryl told me about the types of hamburgers they cooked before asking for my favourite ingredient.

'Beetroot,' I replied, while contemplating poor Judith's obvious problem. 'You've gotta have beetroot . . . and onions.'

Judith returned, a little unsteady on her feet. She didn't say much after that. I wondered if I should suggest taking her home, however some of her friends came over, inviting her to join them. I suspected they took it upon themselves to keep an eye on her at these occasions.

'She'll be fine with us, Amy. You enjoy yourself,' the well-meaning woman told me.

At that point, two couples began dancing. Judith's eyes lit up.

'I wanna dance. Come on, Billy, dance with me.'

'You don't want to dance, Judith. You're coming over to sit down with us and have a natter. That's what you said. Didn't she, Bill?'

Her husband nodded as he gently took her arm.

'Did I? Don't remember. Oh well. Come on Billy, Matilda. Lesh sit down and talk.'

I watched as Judith was guided away. By now, there were eight or so couples loosely arranged in a circle doing the Barn Dance to the sounds of *Colonel Bogey* on the record player. Varied groups were clustered around the edges of the hall, some standing, some seated. There were two dogs lying down, watching.

A hand tapped me on the shoulder. I turned to my left, to have the shock of my life when a young guy jumped out from my right.

'Hiya, gorgeous. You're new. Give us a kiss.'

He appeared to be about my age, with the obvious maturity of a dead cabbage. Absolutely great. Not that I'd seen many handsome young blokes in here, yet it seemed I'd drawn the shortest straw, ending up with the town drongo.

I faced my admirer. He was far too close, and the kissing motions of his mouth reminded me of a particularly ugly fish gasping for air. The acne and slicked back hair didn't improve his image. I might not have been that good-looking, but I was sure I could do better than this . . . this *clown*.

'Come on, lady. Just one little kiss.'

I reeled back. The stink of cigarettes always made me gag.

'You're a smoker. Clear off. No way

I'm kissing someone who smells like an ashtray.'

It didn't deter him. As he reached out to pull my body to him, I caught a movement from the corner of my eye.

'The young lady doesn't want you bothering her, mate. I suggest you clear off.'

It seemed I had a knight coming to my rescue. No doubt one of the older men.

'Don't you tell me to clear off. None of your busin ... ' Guppy-face suddenly backed away as we both saw my knight properly. He was ... well, just perfect.

If it were to come to a fight, I'd no doubt the newcomer would have won — not that I wanted any men quarrelling over me. The fish-man was not only four inches shorter, he was also twenty or thirty pounds lighter. Moreover there was a difference in their stance, one hunched over, the other radiating self-confidence.

'Why don't you apologise and leave?'

Fish-man hesitated, quietly said he was sorry, then slunk off towards the door.

I appraised the chivalrous bloke. Despite not generally judging men on appearance, being a Robert Redford lookalike was a major advantage. Besides, he'd already shown he was a gentleman.

'He's gone now. I'll be off, then.'

I stared into his azure eyes. 'You don't need to. Not unless you're here with a girlfriend.'

'I'm not.'

'Well, stay a moment, then. I want to thank you. I'm Amy.'

'Ross. Ross Wilkinson.' He took my hand to kiss it, like in one of those Jane Austen movies. 'It's great to meet you, Amy.'

I blushed. I hated blushing. It gave my feelings away every time. 'I'm the new . . . '

'Teacher. Everyone's aware of that. Quite the super-heroine too, from what I hear. Don't suppose you have a costume and cape hidden under that fetching dress you're wearing?'

I stared down at myself. I doubted the floral frock with its narrow straps could conceal that.

'Anyone would have done the same. Tell me, Mr Ross Wilkinson. What do you do around here?'

I crossed my fingers behind my back, praying that he wouldn't confess to being a farmer.

'I'm a banker.'

'A what? Oh, you work in a bank. Which one?'

'CNC.'

'City and Country? That's mine. I have to change my account to here from Sydney.'

'Come round after school tomorrow, we'll sort you out. Have to be quick, we close at three-thirty.'

'Three-thirty?' No wonder the term 'bankers' hours' was an insult to a workman. Everyone else finished at five — well, except for teachers.

'In the meantime, Amy, may I have

the pleasure of this dance?'

'You may. Shall we?'

* * *

We spent the rest of the Australia Day
Dance together. Ross kept asking about
me and my life. He was genuinely
interested. From my meagre experience
so far in the dating game, that trait was
a refreshing change. Most guys only
wished to rabbit on about themselves
and, in one case, all his previous
girlfriends, speculating why they'd split
up with him.

To be truthful, we didn't join in every
dance. We'd opted out of the Progres-
sive Barn Dance where you continually
swapped partners. We shared refreshments in the side room instead.

When it was time to leave, Ross and I
strolled onto the street. It wasn't that
late, so I expected there'd be someone
up at my new home. I had my own key
if not. The village hall was about half
way between the school and the

Levinson home.

The night sky was spectacular. Compared to the city with all its lamps, the few street lights here made little difference to the vast vista of stars up there. I pointed out a few constellations to Ross. He recognised the Southern Cross, of course. It was on our flag. He couldn't pick out Orion, though, until I showed him.

We'd already agreed to go to the Platypus Milk-bar after I sorted my paperwork out at his bank the following day.

'Amy,' he said as we held hands. 'I really like you. I'm wondering if perhaps you'd like to go to the pictures in Leeton this Saturday? They're playing *Cactus Flower*.'

My enthusiasm betrayed me.

'With Goldie Hawn? I love Goldie Hawn. Yes. I'd really like that.'

My first date — and with such a dreamboat.

'I've got my own car. A Fiat.'

Naturally. Was I the only person in

Gurawang without transport?

'Which one?'

'The 850 coupé. Only bought it last week.' It was quite sporty. Obviously Ross was doing all right, money-wise. 'Can I walk you home?'

We began sauntering along the edge of the road as there were no footpaths. Ross was closer to the grass verge.

The night was quiet and beautiful. I pointed to a shooting star. Behind me, I heard a car coming and made to walk closer to the fence when I felt Ross grab my waist, pulling me off the road completely. We tumbled onto some grass as a speeding car sped by, missing us by inches. It was gone in an instant, spewing gravel behind it.

'You OK?' Ross asked as we dusted ourselves off. 'Some drunken idiot. Could have killed us.'

'Yeah, I'm all right. Thanks for saving me.'

Was it a drunken idiot? I'd noticed the rear number plate lamp had been blacked out.

'Ross?' I felt his arms wrap around me as our lips touched. My mind told me to be careful — yet right now, I needed someone to love.

6

I was up early, too nervous to sleep any longer. The Levinsons wished me luck as I set off with the same case I'd taken to school as a student. Scary to believe it was little over two years since I'd sat my final high school exams. Was I ready for this? Especially on top of the chaotic ups and downs since I'd arrived in Gurawang.

Last night's near miss with the car hadn't calmed my nerves. On the plus side, I'd met Ross — and that lingering last kiss filled my heart with high expectations for our budding relationship.

I'd decided to dress in a demure matching dress and blouse, rather than slacks. They were a daffodil yellow, reflecting my euphoric emotions. I'd tried to fasten my unruly hair in a bow. After five minutes of struggling, I gave up. Why should my hair behave better than any other day?

There were students joining me on my way, distinctive in their khaki and white uniforms. Mostly they kept a discreet distance even though one or two did call out a friendly, 'Hello, Miss'.

Passing the village hall, I went over the near accident in my mind. The so-and-so might have been smart enough to remove the number plate lamp, but he hadn't reckoned on me recognising the distinctive circular rear light cluster. He was driving an early model Cortina and I was darn certain there weren't too many of them around.

Arriving at my new school, I found myself with another load of introductions. I tried to remember the main ones for me — the other high school teachers. At nine o'clock the bell rang and I followed the other staff into the playground for a start-of-year assembly. It was amazing to see the variation in age and height; from five to sixteen years, from almost microscopic to over six foot.

Colin did his bit before calling me up onto the veranda where he introduced me. It was embarrassing, though worse was to come. From a room behind me, Sharon emerged with Doreen accompanying her. Sharon had a beautiful bouquet of flowers. There was some speech about my effort to save Sharon which I tried not to listen to, as I found it too embarrassing. I didn't want all of this, everyone clapping and cheering. I felt that I was in super-blush mode, my face probably being the colour of Santa Claus' suit.

Sharon gave me the flowers as I bent down to hug her. She whispered in my ear. 'Don't worry Miss. I won't tell that you said the 'b' word.' Then she kissed my cheek.

*　*　*

My first double lesson was to eleven and twelve year olds; their first proper science class.

125

'In science, you need to observe carefully, like a detective,' I explained. Then I requested three volunteers come to the front so I could show them what I meant. 'I'm going to tell you one special thing about each of you that I couldn't possibly know except if I observed you carefully.'

They lined up as the class watched. I read the name tags I'd asked them to wear until I learned their names. The next step was to produce a Sherlock Holmes-type magnifying glass and make a show of using it on my volunteers.

'David. Someone gave you a lift to school.'

'True. But that's an easy guess, Miss. You could have watched Mum drop me off.'

I was undeterred. 'Laura. You were born between July twenty-second and August twenty-first.'

'That's true, Miss Shaw. My birthday is the first of August. How did you guess that?'

'I'll tell you in a moment. Finally let's find out about you, Philip. Hmmm . . . You're a difficult one. Let me check you out. I have to be a real detective now . . . searching for evidence.' I took my time examining him for dramatic effect. 'Ah-ah. Here's a clue. Philip, do you have a baby at your home and did you help with the feeding this morning?'

'That's amazing, Miss Shaw! My baby sister. And yeah, I fed her when Mum was making my sarnies for lunch.'

'Could anyone tell me what I observed?'

No one answered.

'David had a lift because there's no dust on his shoes. Laura's astrology sign is Leo, so I was positive when she was born. She's wearing a Leo necklace.' Laura held up the small silver lion. 'And finally Philip and his baby sister? Philip, I'm afraid you have some vomit on your front.'

Philip looked down. 'Ohhh — my best shirt!'

The class burst into laughter. I'd proved my point.

'Right, class. Your turn. I'm giving you candles to burn and I'd like you to be detectives and write down what you can notice in your school books.'

At first, their results were basic but expanded with a little prompting.

'Use all your senses. Smell? Hearing? Are there different parts to the flame? Colour, shape? What happens when it goes out?'

At the finish of the lesson we discussed their results. Between us, we made fifty points. I was impressed and told them so.

Lunchtime found me on playground duty. I had my hat on to try and protect my freckled skin. Mum once said that too much sun gave complexions like mine more freckles.

Of course I was only six at the time so it was probably one of those Mum-made-up stories but over the years I'd often wondered if it were true. I certainly had my share of the little so-and-sos. If I were a dog, my name would have been Spot.

The kids were all well-behaved, running around like they had energy to spare. Then I noticed one boy sitting on a bench, staring at a line of stones on the wooden table.

I went over, nonchalantly. He looked up.

'Hello, Miss Shaw.'

I'd seen him in one of my classes. Couldn't recall his name, though I did remember he sat by himself the whole lesson, not saying a thing.

'What are you doing there?'

'Studying them.' He produced a book on rocks and minerals. 'I understand a lot about rocks. This one's Narrabeen shale from the Sydney Basin and that's vesicular basalt.'

'Basalt? Not from around here, then?'

'No. Mount Gambier in South Australia. It used to be a volcano. My dad brings me rocks from all over. He's a long distance lorry driver.'

The boy clearly was a geology fan, as

the book he had was quite advanced.

'What's your name?' I asked. He was tall, thin and had his hair cut short, probably by his mum. His clothes were too small, a victim of puberty.

'Stanley.'

'Do you have any friends, Stanley?'

He hesitated.

'My best mate is Graham, who disappeared. He used to bring me loads of rocks and stuff he found with his grandpa.'

The end-of-lunch bell rang; time for afternoon classes. A double art, then a free period. Quickly I ate the last of my Vegemite sandwich.

'Come on, Stanley. Time for lessons.'

He packed his collection away and we went our separate ways — I to my first art lesson ever, and he to metalwork.

★ ★ ★

'Who reckons they can't draw?' was my first question to the girls.

Half the class put their hand up. So did I. They all cheered.

'I'd love to be a brilliant artist but I'm a science teacher. However, I love drawing and painting even though I don't think I'm much good.'

'So do I, Miss.'

I showed them photos of some Picasso and Warhol as well as Kandinski and told them their current value. As expected, they drew comments.

'I can draw a can of soup like that, Miss. Of course I'd have to eat it first and I hate tomato,' Laura the Leo said.

'What are we going to do, Miss? Mr Knovak made us draw boring stuff, like tables or chairs.'

Mr Knovak was the teacher who'd resigned.

'Today, class, I'd like you to draw or paint whatever you like. I want to see what you can do and, if I can help you with some suggestions, would that be OK? You can paint, or use pencils or just do a pen drawing.'

'Anything? Even fairies?'

'Even fairies.'

I watched their positive reaction. Gradually I'd teach perspective and shadows as well as proportions for faces and bodies; however, right now, I needed enthusiasm and self-confidence. Moreover I wanted them to look forward to art lessons and not regard them as boring.

While they worked away I checked out their work, offering both encouragement and ideas for improvement. In between, I sorted through last year's folders of each student's efforts. When I came across a folder with a boy's name on, I was puzzled. All the art students were girls.

'That missing boy, Graham. What's his surname?'

'Robinson, Miss.'

'Thanks, Maissie.' So this folder belonged to the kidnapped boy. 'Why is it here when Graham is a primary student?' I asked the class.

'Mr Knovak used to see Graham a lot after school to help him with lessons,' one of the girls told me.

I arranged Graham's drawings on my bench; horses, superheroes, cars and a painting of a bushranger robbing a stage coach. Underneath Graham had neatly printed *Captain Starlight*. The next two pictures were also of Captain Starlight, rustling cattle and robbing a bank.

Interesting, I thought. Obviously Graham had become fascinated by Gurawang's historical past. I put the folder in my case to pass onto Doreen when I next saw her.

There were fifteen minutes to the bell.

'Right, girls. Tidy up now, and let's see what masterpieces you have to show us all. After that, I'll tell you a story about two girls who drew fairies that looked so real on the photographs they took, that people thought they actually existed.'

Arthur Conan Doyle again. He may have invented Sherlock Holmes but back around 1920, these girls' photos had hoodwinked him completely in a famous story from England called *The Cottingley Fairies*.

★   ★   ★

After school finished, I rushed down to the bank. I had two reasons. The official one was to open my account here so that I could pay in my wages. The second was Ross. Definitely a compelling combination.

Ross had prepared the paperwork which would be sent to my old bank then back again. He advised me in his most professional manner that it would take a week. Finally, he gave me my new passbook which I opened with a five-dollar note.

Ross was dressed very smartly in a white nylon shirt and dark blue tie with matching trousers. I couldn't wait to tell him how great my first day was. I'd taken a coloured photo with my Polaroid of the flowers sitting on my front desk.

'What sort of vase is that?' he asked.

'I didn't have a vase so I used a thousand mil beaker. Being a science teacher has privileges.'

I waited around outside the bank until he'd finished up with the till. It was only about ten minutes. Meanwhile, I'd checked out the main street — or what there was of it — saying hello to the odd passer-by.

When he came out he gave me a quick kiss on the cheek. We walked around to The Platypus Milk-bar where we could sit and chat. Beryl came over for our order.

'Do you have banana milkshakes?' I asked.

'Banana? I'm afraid not, love. Strawberry, vanilla and chocolate.'

'No thanks. I'll have a Passiona. Oh, and a cake, please.'

'Well, we have some lamingtons and . . . '

'A lammie please. I love lammies.' I smiled all the time she took Ross' order. Life was great even if they didn't have my favourite flavour. I had a theory that civilisation started where they served banana milkshakes. Everywhere else was the back of Burke. It wasn't a great recommendation for my new home in one way — yet, at that moment, I felt so great.

'You had a good first day, Amy? Tell me all about it.'

I was about to, until I remembered that Moriarty was still out there — and my list of people I could trust didn't include Ross. At least, not yet.

'It was fantastic. The other teachers were fantastic and the kids were all especially fantastic,' I enthused.

Ross grinned. 'It was OK, then?'

'How about yours?'

'I'd prefer to discuss you, kitten. Nothing wrong with that, is there?'

He'd asked the question, so I thought about it. I'd virtually told him everything about me and my life, yet I was in the dark about him, apart from his name and workplace. I didn't have a clue about Ross Wilkinson and somehow that didn't seem right in any type of relationship. Nonetheless he was attentive and handsome so I decided to enjoy the moment.

Nothing beats a Passiona and a lammie — that is, except a banana shake and a lammie. I took my time with the chocolate and coconut-covered sponge slice, sipping the passionfruit soft drink as I ate.

Staring at Ross' boyish face with his neatly combed-back hair, I reached across to ruffle it a little. Big mistake.

'What are you doing, Amy?' he almost shouted. The other customers seated at their Formica tables glanced at us. I stammered an apology. I was simply feeling good about us.

Ross' reaction reminded me about that day I wanted to pat a Tassie devil in a nature park north of Sydney. I think I was eight. My mum explained it wasn't a good idea. We watched the 'cute' little animals rip into their food at mealtime and I could see exactly what Mum meant.

In a moment, the old smiling, butter-wouldn't melt Ross was back. No word of regret though.

'You looking forward to Saturday night, Amy? Should be a fab movie.'

'Yeah,' I said automatically before thinking about it. I was really keen to see it, and it was simply a date. What could go wrong? I smiled at Ross. 'Did I tell you I love Goldie Hawn?'

'I think you mentioned it six or seven times.'

'I have to go back to school now to prepare for lessons. Will I see you tomorrow after work?'

'Unfortunately, no. I'm on holidays all week from now on. My parents' anniversary. I'll be back Saturday arvo ready to pick you up around six.'

As Beryl came to clear away our plates and glasses, Ross gave her money.

'A fifty? I can't cash that, young man.'

I wasn't surprised she didn't have change. It was half a week's wages for me.

'I don't have anything smaller, I'm afraid,' he responded with a sorry shrug of the shoulders. I was astounded at that. He worked in a blinking bank and should realise that not many people would use fifty dollar notes.

I took my purse out and flipped the catch.

'I'll pay, Beryl. And could I please have some milk and a box of Winning Post?'

Mrs L had asked for the milk. The choccies in that distinctive green box had been around since I was a kid and were a classic assortment. They were a present for the Levinsons. I was certain they'd enjoy them and, if not, I knew someone else who would.

I felt a bit angry at Ross putting me in this awkward position. He was aware I didn't have a lot of cash until my first pay cheque came through.

'Oh, I'll take those jelly packets on the shelf, please,' he said. 'Only the mandarin ones.'

'All of them?' Beryl asked. No one

likes that flavour except . . . '

'Amy. Could you pay, please? I'll give you the money on Saturday.'

I took another two dollars from my rapidly emaciating purse.

'Thanks, beautiful. I owe you one,' he said.

We parted outside the shop. I wasn't feeling so happy any more. Was Saturday night at the pictures a good idea, or would I find myself out of pocket again?

★   ★   ★

Soon after arriving back at the Levinson's, Kyle rang with an update.

'I interviewed that American railway worker. It seems he's not involved, at least not directly. He was working when the explosion occurred, a hundred miles from here. He was aware of the gelignite being stored in the van and might have mentioned it to others but can't recall who. He fancies the amber nectar a bit too much from what I can gather. Unfortunately he wasn't in Australia when Graham was kidnapped.'

The American involvement still seemed likely to me with the misspelling of 'moralizing'.

'Forgot to ask, Amy. How was your first day?'

'The school part was great,' I told him. I didn't mention the disappointment with Ross. 'I guess you and Tuesday are getting ready for dinner.'

'Tuesday's still out. She enjoys going walkabout down the creek. I'll wait till she's home before getting our meals. When are you going to take up that offer for tea with us? Saturday night?'

I thought of the pictures and Ross.

'Sorry. I'm busy. Next week, perhaps?'

'Whenever. I told her all about you, by the way.'

I could imagine. Kyle probably thought of me as a girl who was helping him out rather than anyone that might be special.

There wasn't much to report from my feeble efforts at investigating so I didn't prolong our conversation. The discoveries that Graham had a friend who studied stones and that he was a fan of long-dead bushrangers weren't going to help.

The phone call finished, I went to find Mr L. He was outside locking up the chooks for the night.

As I reached the screen door, I could see him in the garden. Unsteady on his feet, he grabbed at a tall bush to support him. It collapsed. He tumbled onto a wheelbarrow and didn't move.

I called to Mrs L in the kitchen behind me.

'Cyril's fallen over. Ring for the doctor.'

It was a split-second decision. The doctor was much closer, only a hundred feet away in the next house. The ambos might be needed but they'd take much longer. I hoped Mrs L wouldn't panic, trusting that I'd go to the aid of her hubby.

He wasn't moving. I knelt down beside him.

'Cyril? Cyril? Can you hear me?'

7

Mr L started to raise his head. 'Wha . . . what happened? Amy? Is that you?'

He was staring past me, seemingly unable to make my features out clearly. I put his fallen glasses into his hand, checking for any obvious injuries. Thankfully, he appeared OK apart from some scratches. Even with his glasses on, he remained disorientated. There was no way I could lift him, but perhaps if we both tried?

'Take it easy, Cyril. I'm here.'

'That you, Doc? Sounds like you.'

The doctor knelt down next to us. Mrs L was watching, wringing her hands in concern.

'He's not seeing so well,' I explained. We were in dark shadow now as the sun was setting.

'Come on, old friend. Let's get you inside.'

The doctor's comforting manner was exactly what was needed. I sensed Cyril might have had problems for some weeks yet kept them to himself for some typically male reason.

Mr L accepted our help gratefully as we both gently lifted him to his feet.

Once inside, Doctor MacAlister went to retrieve his Gladstone bag from the hall where he'd left it.

'Don't fuss, Mother,' Mr L protested.

'I'll fuss if I want, you silly old galah.'

Cyril was seated on the settee. He didn't notice Mrs L turn her back to shed a few tears of relief. I gave her a hug as the doc opened his bag.

'Keep the heid, Cyril. Keep calm. Let's have a proper look at you. Don't keep any secrets from me. You owe it to Miriam to let me sort you out.'

I guided Mrs L to the kitchen.

'Perhaps we should give them some privacy. How about I make us all a nice cup of tea?'

Mrs L sat down and nodded.

'How long have you and Mr L been married?'

'Fifty years in September. We married young — you did in those days. Just after the Great War. Never wanted anyone else in my life. We have our spats, but who doesn't? I love him, and he says he loves me. When I saw him lying out there . . . '

'Here. Here's your tea. Careful, it's hot.'

We sat together until the doc came out to us.

'How bad is it, Hamish?' Mrs L asked.

'Not bad at all. He's a tough old laddie. Have you noticed anything wrong with Cyril lately?'

'A bit unsure on his feet. You saw that too, didn't you, Amy?'

I nodded, preparing cups for him and Cyril.

'Cataracts. He can't see well. We can fix him up right as rain. A simple operation at the hospital. It's like he's seeing everything through a dense fog.

Be worse at night, I would think.'

Hence his reluctance to drive in the dark.

Mrs L appeared puzzled.

'He had a proper check-up at the hospital last month. Surely they would have seen it and told you. I'm positive they did an eye examination.'

The jovial grey-haired doctor went pale.

'Oh my Lord. I've done something terrible.'

'You, Hamish? I can't believe that. You're a brilliant doctor.'

He slumped onto the table. I could see he was upset, presumably at something he'd not done.

'No excuses, Miriam — however, you remember what happened? With Morag?'

'Of course I do, Hamish. A dreadful thing. We were so shocked by her passing, especially being a tragic accident.'

I was struggling a little with his accent. Scottish, I thought. Or Welsh?

'Morag used to look after the paperwork for me in the surgery. I thought I was coping well but clearly not. I can recall a letter from Leeton Hospital arriving . . . I think it's there, with the other mail. I haven't opened most of it.'

The clues were there. His suit trousers weren't pressed, his shirt and tie were both dirty. Just like Mr L, our local doctor had been struggling though he had been too proud to admit it.

Trying his best to make up for the oversight, the doctor immediately rang the hospital then the ophthalmic surgeon at home. Cyril's initial appointment was made for the next day although he was forbidden to drive himself. As Mrs L couldn't drive at all, she checked with her daughter-in-law on the phone. Tracey was only too happy to help.

'I'm so sorry, Miriam,' Hamish confessed once the arrangements were finalised. 'I've let you both down.'

'No real harm done. Apart from

breaking that bush when Cyril fell. Between you and me, Hamish, I hated that bush.'

Mrs L understood it wasn't appropriate to make the doctor feel any worse than he already did.

They went inside to explain everything to Cyril in detail, including the operation. Once finished, I accompanied the doctor to the front door.

'I don't believe I thanked you properly for the other night, Doctor MacAlister.'

'Call me Hamish, please, Amy.'

'I wanted a word myself. I don't want to intrude but it sounds like you require assistance at the surgery. I might know a person who could help.'

'I'd be stupid not to consider it in the circumstances. Who is it ye have in mind?'

'She's a trained nurse, great at organisation.'

'Great. Who is she?'

'Judith.' I saw his expression change. 'From the school.'

'Hmmm. Not sure about her because of . . .'

'Her problem? I believe a lot of that is down to boredom. Perhaps you might help one another? Please?'

'You're persistent. OK. If she's interested and if it's acceptable to that husband of hers, ask her to call tomorrow after surgery. Around three o'clock. No promises, though.'

I jumped up to kiss him on the cheek.

'You're a star, Doc . . . er, Hamish.'

Now he was the one to blush.

When I returned to the lounge, Mrs L grinned.

'I overheard your plan, Amy. Two birds with one stone? And it just might work at that.'

★   ★   ★

There was a fab song by the Easybeats back in 1966 — *Friday on My Mind*. It was about a guy looking forward to finishing work on Friday because he

150

hated the other days.

Based on my first day teaching, I'd love weekdays. Nonetheless I was really anticipating finishing work on Friday because I'd be able to bank my first ever pay cheque. Fantastic. It might be a few days after until I could draw any money out, but that didn't stop this Friday being super-duper special for me.

Mr L seemed fine on Wednesday morning, relieved that his problem could be sorted out.

'I was imagining all sorts of things, Miriam. I realised I couldn't see so well, but you were relying on me so I didn't say anything to you.'

'I say what I think, Father. You gave me such a scare. Right now, I think you've behaved like the dumbest wombat in the world.'

He gave a sheepish grin.

'I assume that's worse than a silly old galah?'

'Lots worse, Father.' Then she leaned over the dining table to kiss his forehead. 'We need to get ready. Tracey will be here at nine-thirty.'

★ ★ ★

My lessons on Wednesday and Thursday went smoothly. I was learning the names of my classes very quickly. Specialist teachers came two days a week to instruct the kids in metalwork, woodwork and needlework. That left three permanent teachers, including Colin, to handle maths, English, history, social studies and geography.

One amazing thing in my favour was the response of the kids to my teaching. Like every other science teacher I'd met, I allowed the kids to do experiments in class. That hadn't been the case with my predecessor, Mr Knovak — he'd demonstrated everything on the front bench. It made for a lot more class control, though much less fun and actual hands-on learning for the students. I was amazed to discover that none of them, not even the oldest children, had learned how to use a Bunsen burner.

I was finding a routine. Staying after school when students and most teachers had gone home allowed me two hours to prepare lessons for the following day. I worked around the cleaner and made sure I locked up and left before she was finished. Given the situation on my arrival, I preferred not to be totally on my own.

In any case I was looking forward to Friday for another reason — tennis. I enjoyed playing and despite not being brilliant at it like Evonne Goolagong, I was fast and had a powerful serve. Hopefully I'd be good enough for my first session the following evening. I'd heard that Judith and Barbara Fletcher, the Reverend's wife, were strong players. Kyle was on our team also.

A knock on the classroom door at four-thirty on Thursday gave me a start. Outside the screen door were two girls and an older man with receding hair. I taught one of the girls, Kerrie-Anne.

The man had a newspaper clutched in one hand.

'G'day. Can I help you?' I asked.

'Hello, Miss Shaw. I'm Peter Gilmore. You've met Kerrie-Anne. This is Rhonda. Wondered if I could introduce myself proper? I'm President of the Local P and C.' It was the voluntary organisation of parents and citizens set up to support most schools, often with fundraising.

My mind filed through all the names I'd heard. *Peter Gilmore? Peter Gilmore?* Then it came back to me; Mrs L had mentioned that name, closely followed by 'thieving' and 'sheep droppings'. He ran the local farm supply shop.

I held out my hand to him and Rhonda.

'Pleased to meet you both.'

Rhonda said nothing although she gave me a warm smile before sidling up to her father as if frightened of being too far away from him.

'Have a seat. Please call me Amy. Not

Kerrie-Anne, though; I'm Miss Shaw to you, young lady.'

I needed to maintain a teacher-pupil distance, especially in this close-knit community.

Mr Gilmore wasn't interested.

'No thanks, Miss Shaw. I wanted to introduce myself on Tuesday only to find you'd left at three on the dot. Not very impressed, I must say.'

I crossed my arms defensively.

'I had my reasons and I did return for two hours later that day. You can check the time book if you wish, although I'm quite certain I'm not responsible to you.'

That'll put you in your place, you arrogant dill, I thought. I felt as though we were competing, scoring points in a game of tennis.

Gilmore love, Shaw fifteen.

'Doesn't matter, lovey. You're here now.' I clenched my fist. 'Lovey' was right up there with 'girlie' on my list of insults. The bloke clearly had tickets on himself.

What was worse, he'd brought his daughters to witness his arrogance towards me and, by extension, towards women in general. If he had his way, Aussie women would still be denied the right to vote.

'You're a real Meggsie, aren't you, Miss Shaw?' was his next remark.

I flexed my biceps. This bloke was pushing his luck. He either had a few kangaroos loose in the top paddock or he was deliberately trying to wind me up. I suspected it was the latter. Calling me a Meggsie was a reference to a comic strip called *Ginger Meggs* in the Sunday Telegraph. It was about a boy with red hair and I'd had my share of that nickname as a pupil in school. There was no way I'd put up with it as a teacher.

'Thanks, Mr Gilmore. Professor Meggs always said I was going to follow in his footsteps as a great teacher. I didn't realise you'd heard of him out here in the sticks.' I watched his expression change to anger.

Gilmore love, Shaw thirty.

He brandished the rolled-up paper in my face.

'I came to discuss this. Front page. Not the type of publicity that I'd like for this school.'

'I haven't seen the weekly paper yet, Mr Gilmore. May I?'

There was a photo of me carrying Sharon as we ran from the burning pub. It seemed someone had taken it, although I'd not noticed at the time. I'd had other things on my mind. The headline read *Saved from Explosion.*

I scanned it quickly.

'I don't understand, Mr Gilmore. This is reasonably factual and doesn't mention my profession or the school. What's your problem?'

'Everyone here is aware of what your job is. It reflects badly. See here? They call you a *red devil wielding an axe.*'

I'd had enough of his pathetic tirade.

'I saved Sharon. I can't be responsible for what some reporter writes. If you'd been there instead of me it might have read *grey devil wielding an axe*. Or are you the type of person who watches while others do the hard work?'

Gilmore love, Shaw forty.

Mr Gilmore touched his hair. Amazingly, it moved. Just a little. I stared, perceiving the slight colour variation where reality ceased and make-believe began. He was wearing a wig.

I grinned — and, seeing that grin, Mr Let's-Have-A-Go-At-Meggsie-Shaw Gilmore realised that I was privy to his vain secret.

Game, Set and Match to Amy Shaw.

I chose not to say anything about his hairpiece. Leave your enemy some dignity in defeat and he will appreciate that. A life-lesson Dad taught me.

'I'll . . . I'll be keeping an eye on you, Miss Shaw. In the meantime I wanted to wish you all the best as a teacher here. Come on, girls. Time to go.'

I sat down. First Moriarty and his efforts to intimidate me; now Mr G with his trained hairpiece. Did I appear to be some docile pushover due to my diminutive size?

After a few minutes Colin knocked and entered.

'You survived, then, Amy? I'm sorry, I was down the road. Judith told me the minute I returned.'

'You could have warned me. I felt like a female Doctor Who facing the wrath of the Daleks.'

'He's a bit full-on at times but he does great things raising money for the school. He personally put new basketball posts up in the holidays. By the way, Judith was extremely pleased with your recommendation and so, it seems, is the doctor. She did mention she may have let slip a comment about zombies that she made the other night?'

'Did she? I can't remember. Can't have been important. In any case, I'm here to teach, not gossip. I like Judith and I hope she likes mc. The same goes for you, even if you are my boss.'

'She wants to make sure you haven't forgotten the tennis at seven tomorrow.

There's a spare racket and sports kit if you need one.'

'Oh yeah, tennis. I just had a practice session with Mr Gilmore — metaphorically speaking. I'll take her up on the racket, thanks. Best be off. I want to check how Mr L is after his hospital visit.'

'Mr L? Oh, Mr Levinson. Give him our regards. See you tomorrow, Amy. Your first pay-day.'

'Is it? I didn't realise,' I said with a wink.

★　★　★

Friday came at last. Since I wasn't on playground duty, I rushed over to the bank to deposit my cheque at lunchtime. It was a brilliant feeling.

The afternoon was sports lessons. I took the girls for volleyball along with Pauline, the maths teacher. She umpired while I joined in playing. Fortunately we were under the shade of some humungous pine trees or I might have ended up sunburned again.

As I waited outside the school for the buses and parents to take the kids home, I was approached by Laura the Leo.

'My big sis wants to speak to you, Miss Shaw. It's a bit private.'

Laura hung back while I wandered off with a girl about my age. She was pretty and, like me, seemed fairly self-confident.

'My name's Gail. I wanted a quiet word about Ross. The gossip is that you're going out with him. The pictures? Tomorrow?'

'I didn't realise it was common knowledge.'

'It's not. Ross is . . . well, predictable. And, despite initial impressions, he's not a nice bloke.'

'Go on. I assume he's taken you out?'

'Yeah. A few weeks ago. Pictures at Leeton. Saturday night. Stopped at a picnic spot on the way back. That's when he became . . . shall we say, amorous. He wouldn't stop when I asked him to so I got out of that sports car of his. He told me to let him ... you know ... or he'd leave me there. It was eleven at night. When I told him to get stuffed, he drove off. Good thing I wasn't far from my auntie's and that it was a full moon. Still took me forty minutes to walk to her place.'

Gail began to cry. I gave her my hankie.

'I've done things with boys before, but not that. I wanted my first time to be special and not like that. I hate him for what he tried to do. Worse still, he dumped me without a care. It's not only me. There's half a dozen girls he's done that to. From what I hear, one or two were so scared that they ... let him. Not everyone's strong as me.'

I was shocked. She was discussing my Ross.

Gail dried her eyes.

'Why do you think he asked you, Amy? Sorry. That came out wrong. You're really beautiful, not like me. The main reason he asked you so quick is because you might hear about him if he waited. None of the local girls want anything to do with him. Laura says you're nice, so I'm warning you.'

She seemed genuine. Her tears had stopped.

'Why not tell someone?' I asked her. 'The police? Your parents?'

'His word against ours? What's the point? Gurawang's not like the Big Smoke. If you're a girl and you get a reputation out here, no one lets you forget it. And it's always the girls' fault, leading the blokes on with their lippy and short dresses. Anyways, I've done my bit. What you do now . . . I guess that's up to you.'

I thanked Gail, even if I found what she said about my Ross impossible to believe. We hugged and she left with Laura, getting into a Holden ute.

I decided to go home. I still found it hard to conceive. Ross came across as a real catch and he'd saved me from Fish-features as well as from being squished by that Cortina. Nevertheless, there was that odd situation at the milk-bar; expecting me to pay for everything. Even those blinking jellies. That was bizarre in itself. What grown bloke eats jellies and why did he want so many? Was he doing a huge trifle for his parent's anniversary? Not blinking likely.

★ ★ ★

Mrs L had a favour to ask when I arrived back.

'I realise it's your weekend, Amy, but we're wondering if you could drive us to Leeton tomorrow for shopping. Normally Cyril drives but now, till he's had his operation, we're stuck a bit.'

'No worries. I wanted a look round anyway. I've heard about a picnic spot on the Leeton Road.'

'You want a picnic on the way back?'

'No. It's something one of the other girls told me about my date with Ross

164

from the bank. I'm probably going to cancel it.'

'Oh, that would be a shame. I've heard it's a fine movie. *Cactus Blossom*, or something. Vince and Tracey are going to see it tomorrow night. Vince loves movies.'

So Vince and Tracey were going to watch *Cactus Flower*. A plan was beginning to form in my brain. Maybe I would go with darling Ross after all.

'Sorry, Mrs L. Miles away. You were saying that Vince enjoys going to the pictures?'

'He loves all the stars. Names the farm animals after them. You've met Marilyn and there's Brigitte, the cattle dog, after Brigitte Bardot. Course he didn't realise Brigitte was male.'

'Probably explains why that dog is so darn neurotic,' Mr L piped up. 'Barking mad, if you ask me. Get it?' Mrs L gave him a disapproving stare yet I couldn't stop a snigger at his joke.

It was good to see he was coping OK with being banned from wandering around alone. I'd volunteered to collect the eggs each morning and look after the chooks until he was fit once again.

'Excuse me. I wonder if I could give Vince and Tracey a ring. I have a favour to ask them.'

'No need, sweetheart. They're pulling up in the driveway right now.'

Good. I had plans for Mr Ross Wilkinson. And if he expected another Saturday night love-in, he'd be in for a painful surprise.

8

The Gurawang tennis courts were state-of-the-art. Clearly the locals enjoyed the game. There were four floodlit courts, as well as a spacious glass-fronted covered area for spectators.

Right now, that's where I was. Judith and I had teamed up for two matches, and were sitting this one out. All the courts were full with non-players umpiring.

Judith was alert and sober. She confessed she'd struggled with a lack of things to do; a few hours as school secretary was far from fulfilling.

'I didn't drink all the time, though I'm aware I had a reputation as a lush. I have a low tolerance for alcohol so one drink for me is like three for most people. Something to do with enzymes. I do have a problem, though, and I intend to change. Hamish is doing hypnotherapy to support me.'

She stared at her hands as she opened up to me. I felt certain that we would become friends.

She stood up, moving closer to the window to watch a long rally on the nearest court.

'Hamish actually suggested that I might find a role as a sort of district nurse, visiting new mothers and giving injections at home rather than expecting patients to come into the surgery all the time. He's investigating the funding. Once again, thanks for recommending me. I never thought about approaching him. Don't know why.'

'I'm glad I could help, Judith. Obviously I never met his wife . . . Morag? What was she like?'

'Lovely person. Always ready to lend a hand. She and Mrs Levinson were organising a huge Christmas party for all their friends and relatives. That never happened, of course. Very tragic.'

'I gather it was an accident?'

Judith sipped her coffee. I had a cup

of tea. I found coffee too bitter, even with sugar.

'Car accident. Killed instantly, apparently.'

I nodded sombrely. It was clear why Hamish had been struggling. I decided to change the subject, choosing to include Judith in my list of confidants about young Graham.

'Judith — I'd prefer you keep what I'm going to tell you secret between you and Colin for the moment, but Kyle and I have reason to believe that Graham was kidnapped from the creek. They found chloroform at the crime scene.'

'Kidnapped? Why would whoever it was, take a nine-year-old? It . . . it simply doesn't make sense. Are Doreen and Big Jim aware of this theory?'

'Yes. Furthermore I've had threats to stay out of the investigation. No idea who's behind it all. Someone local, I expect. There are some puzzling developments that you might be able to shed some light on.'

'Such as?' I had her full attention.

'Such as where would Moriarty get chloroform? And before you ask, Moriarty's the made-up name Mr Levinson gave the bad guy.'

'Doctor's surgery? Vet? Your lab? I do the stock-take each year. You've got some nasty chemicals there, Amy. Potassium cyanide for starters, white phosphorus, sodium. Potassium. Concentrated hydrochloric and sulphuric acids Should I go on?'

'No, I'm aware. And I checked the chloroform. Two bottles . . . full. Just like the inventory.'

'I'll examine Doctor MacAlister's stock tomorrow although I suspect Senior Constable Travis has already done that. Have you noticed how handsome our local copper is?'

Someone else match-making? Kyle had a wife. I wasn't into breaking up anyone's marriage.

'Kyle's not my type, Judith. Moving on. There's another puzzle you might have suggestions about. Captain Starlight?'

'Who mentioned the Captain?'

It was Barbara from the Sunday School.

'No one,' I replied on impulse. 'We were simply talking about the . . . captivating starry night.'

Judith stared at me in horror.

'It was the best I could come up with,' I whispered with a shrug. 'I don't want the whole blinking town to find out.'

'Amy. Her husband is a minister, she runs the local Sunday School. I really think she's one of the good guys, don't you?'

'Guess you're right,' I admitted weakly.

Judith tutted. 'Honestly, kiddo. You mostly seem so cluey but other times you're off with the fairies. Sorry.'

'No, I am a dozy duck at times. Too many freckles. They interfere with my brain.' *Especially when it comes to smooth-talking blokes called Ross,* I thought. 'Barbara. Welcome to our club of amateur detectives. I'm

Batgirl. She's Robin.'

'Why are you Batgirl?'

'My ears are bigger. What do you know about Captain Starlight?'

'Everything, Amy. Absolutely everything. But first fill me in on what we're detectiving.'

'Detectiving? There's no such word.' Judith threw her arms in the air. 'I'm surrounded by dozy ducks. There's feathers everywhere.'

Between us, we brought Barbara up to date on the search for Graham — Moriarty, his nasty note, the punctured fuel tank, the chloroform and the biggest question: why kidnap a nine-year-old boy? Barbara listened attentively until we finished.

'So what's Starlight got to do with it?'

'Maybe nothing,' I admitted. 'I'm certain Graham suddenly became interested in him in the weeks before he disappeared. He did paintings and took books about him out of the school library. I checked.'

The tennis games were almost finished.

Barbara began to explain.

'As you probably realise, Captain Starlight was a made-up name in the book *Robbery Under Arms* written in the late 1800s. It's generally thought it was loosely based on the life of Harry Readford and other bushrangers yet I believe otherwise. There was actually a criminal who called himself by that name in the 1860s. His real name was Lion Judah O'Lachlan.'

'Bit of a mouthful,' Judith said. 'Why have I never heard of him?'

'He was the black sheep of the O'Lachlan dynasty. They were big landowners hereabouts, very protective of their status. When Lion did something bad the authorities would blame it on Ned Kelly, Ben Hall, Dan Morgan or Henry Readford. Reputation was everything back then and the local police were happy to hush up Lion's activities for a few shillings. The people around here knew about him, though, and a few wrote about the

Captain in their diaries. That's how I found out about him. I've been writing a book about the history of the area and its people.'

'What did Starlight do?' Judith enquired.

'Anything illegal. Cattle duffing, murder, stage coach robberies, banks, gold from Bendigo. He amassed quite a fortune, I gather.'

The other players were swapping around for the next round of matches. Time for our turn on the court. We grabbed our rackets to join them. We'd finish this conversation later.

'One thing, Barbara. What happened to him?'

'Died penniless of TB in 1882.'

'And the treasure?' My imagination was in overdrive.

'No idea. He certainly never spent it.'

* * *

Saturday morn was hot and sunny. There was talk of heavy storms all week beginning Sunday afternoon. We headed off to Leeton at eight-thirty with me driving. It was the same in Sydney; everywhere closed at twelve for the weekend. The only chance working people had to buy groceries, clothes or virtually anything was late night shopping on Thursday or the mad rush on Saturday morning. I hated it.

'We'll visit your picnic area on the way home, Amy. Probably show you the sights of Leeton after twelve. There's the big fruit canning factory. I guess you've heard of it? Leetona?'

I had. Ate their peaches all my life growing up.

Mr L continued with his tourism speech.

'Then there's the Murrumbidgee. Biggest river around here. Used to be larger still until they built the dams and the weirs. Are you looking forward to that movie tonight?'

'The movie — yes.' The company I'd be in was another thing. I hadn't told the Levinsons about Gail's revelations regarding Ross. I didn't wish to add to their worries at that moment. Vince and Tracey were aware of the full story, though.

'You're invited to Currawong tomorrow if you feel up to it, Amy. Don't feel you have to drive us. It's no problem for Tracey to collect us.'

'No. I'd love to come.' I glanced at the now functioning fuel gauge, pleased that it was full. Mr L had asked the mechanic to repair it and the tank. The Falcon was now kept in their locked garage when not in use, in case of sabotage.

It had been an eventful week since I arrived in Gurawang. I was disappointed we hadn't moved any closer to finding Graham, yet I was hopeful.

★ ★ ★

The Leeton trip wasn't that exciting. Shops were shops wherever you went. True, the ones out here in the remote bush charged higher prices than Bondi. I didn't expect it to be any different this side of the black stump.

Actually that wasn't very fair. People out in this part of New South Wales probably figured the black stump — the outer limit of civilisation — was further out west, just near Woop Woop (even further out in the sticks). It's a matter of perspective — like when my generation reckon forty is old, whereas Mum's generation figure forty is middle-aged and you're not old until you're sixty.

In any case, I was dressed and eager to see *Cactus Flower*. Ross picked me up on time in his expensive sports car. When I asked him about his parents' anniversary, he didn't say much. Surprisingly, he bought the movie tickets, leaving me to buy the popcorn. When I mentioned his promise to reimburse me for Tuesday's snack and his stupid packets of mandarin jelly, he told me he'd fix me up at the end of the night out.

He wasn't as attentive as he had been. That suited me fine. Gail's confession about his behaviour with her and other Gurawang girls had made me realise again how naïve I was at times.

It was ten o'clock when the movie finished. I was disappointed in it. I did notice that Tracey and Vince were up in the dress circle, whereas Ross had chosen the cheapy front stalls.

When he tried to put his arms around me, I complained I was too hot, and anyway we were there to watch the show. Despite him seeming a little put out, he didn't make a fuss. I suspected he was biding his time for the drive back home.

Waiting time was over. We'd been driving for quite a while back on the Leeton Road. No stars were visible through the clouds. Also there were very few cars travelling either way, and the dim lights of roadside homes or farms were rare.

Ross shifted gears down as he slowly braked.

'What are you doing, Ross?'

'I heard a knocking in the engine. I'm pulling up to check there's nothing loose. There's a picnic spot just off the road up here.'

I couldn't hear any sound from the rear-mounted motor. We pulled off onto a dirt track surrounded by trees and picnic tables. There was one other car parked there in the shadows. Its lights were off.

Ross drove well past it before stopping completely. He switched the interior light on but made no move to get out.

'Have to let it cool down first, Amy. In the meantime why don't we get better acquainted?'

'That's a good idea,' I responded, innocently. 'What should we talk about? Star signs, favourite books?'

'I had something else in mind, actually. It won't involve any talking either.' He moved his left hand around my shoulder to my left arm while he leaned over to place his right hand on my neck.

'Will you take your hands away, Ross?'

He didn't. Instead he lifted the top of my blouse away from my skin, in spite of me crossing my arms.

'Doesn't seem like there's much there, but it will have to do for the moment.' He was leering at me now. In the dim light of the single lamp, my 'lovely' Ross appeared more like a freaky monster than a handsome young man.

He forced my arms open and put his hand under the top button.

'Just do what you're told, Amy. Otherwise I'm going to have to hurt you . . . really, really badly.'

9

'I don't think so, mate. You're not getting an eyeful tonight.' I twisted away, grabbing his fingers with one hand and the car keys with the other. As I bent his fingers backwards he screamed out in pain, vainly attempting to squirm away from me. The trouble was he had nowhere to hide; the front bucket seats were too close together.

'Owwww. What . . . oww . . . you doing, Amy? Stop it. OWW. It hurts!'

'It's meant to, Ross. You threatened me, and you touched me when I told you not to. Maybe I should break one of your fingers?'

'No, no, no! Don't do that.'

I released the pressure a little. He lifted his other hand as a fist, starting to king-hit me in the face. Unfortunately for him, I was faster. Pushing down harder on his fingers, I could see the pain in his tear-filled eyes. I opened the car door and edged out, gripping his fingers all the time.

He struggled to speak. 'What are you doing? It was only a bit of a lark. You're a maniac!'

I shouldn't have taken pleasure in this. He was so pathetic. All I could think of was him being here with those other, more defenceless girls, taking advantage of their vulnerability. He had all the cards; his manly strength and the power of having them alone in his car, miles from assistance.

I let go of his fingers which he immediately massaged to ease the hurt. The look in his eyes was pure evil.

He sneered, trying to regain some of his perceived masculine control. No one enjoyed being humiliated and to be reduced to tears by a woman as petite as I was must have really crushed his ego.

'You'll pay for that!' Clearly my former almost-boyfriend was losing his block, letting his raw emotions control him. I felt a little smug; I'd not lost my temper except for one sadistic moment thinking about the others. I was ashamed of that.

'So I suppose there's no chance of a lift back to Gurawang?' I asked, sweetly.

'You're joking, right? I'm leaving you here. You'll have to walk home — if you can find the way, you stupid cow. And as for what I ever saw in you . . . you ugly, spotted, ginger, ungrateful, ugly cow . . . '

The vindictive words hurt but I wouldn't show it.

'You said 'ugly' twice,' I retorted.

'I'm . . . I'm reporting you to the cops. Assault, that's what it was.'

'Your word against mine, darling.'

What followed were tirades of colour-ful swear words, much worse than the 'b' one. It cheapened him even more.

'Anyway, I'm off. Enjoy your walk back, bitch.'

He reached down to turn the key, only to find it wasn't there. He felt around on the floor in the feeble roof light of his coupé.

'These what you're trying to find?'

I dangled the keys outside the passenger window. Although he made a grab for them from inside, I'd stepped back out of reach. Immediately he opened the driver's door and stepped out. I could see his face in the light of the full moon that was now illuminating the area through the scattering clouds. He was manic.

Ross watched in horror as I revisited my days throwing the javelin in the inter-schools athletics competitions. We both watched the hurled keyring sail through the night air, over the car and Ross' upturned face only to disappear into the dense undergrowth more than a hundred feet away.

'No!' he screamed. 'What have you done?'

'What a shame. Now we'll both have to walk home. Or . . . maybe not.' I gave a small hand signal out of Ross' line of sight. Car headlamps came on from behind us on the picnic-spot road. A car engine sprang to life. Within seconds, the vehicle had pulled up next to me, the engine purring away. Ross hadn't budged from his side of the car. Good; I wasn't prepared for a fight with him out in the open.

'You OK, miss?' a deep, masculine voice asked from inside the darkened car interior.

'Actually no. My ex-boyfriend has car problems. He thought there was knocking in the engine but it now appears much more serious. Difficulties starting it, I believe. Could you possibly give me a lift to Gurawang? If it's no trouble?'

'No trouble at all. Hop in the back,' a female voice said from the big Ford Fairlane.

'What . . . what about me?' Ross asked, timidly.

'You said you'd wait here, remember, Ross. Try to fix it? After all, you're so good with those little hands of yours.'

I opened the back door but the car interior stayed dark. Ross couldn't see who my rescuers were, and the rear number plate light wasn't on. It was a trick Cortina Man had taught me. These were precautions if he tried to track my rescuers down, once he worked out that they weren't here by chance. As for white Ford Fairlanes? Every farmer had one.

'Bye, Ross. Thanks for the lovely night out but I'm afraid I won't be going out with you any more.'

We drove off, leaving him wondering what had happened. No doubt he'd find his keys eventually, even if he had to wait until dawn.

'Thanks for that. It was going to get very nasty. I hope you didn't mind waiting there so long?'

'No worries. We used to come here courting ourselves. We had a chance to . . . reminisce.'

I smiled. Even in the darkened car, I could see Tracey's dishevelled hair.

'We heard a lot of shouting and name-calling as well as watching you tossing his keys away. I couldn't believe you did that. Remind me never to ruffle your feathers, Miss School Teacher.'

'Serves the so-and-so right, doing that to those young women.' Vince's voice was measured with an undercurrent of anger. Had she been a few years older, their own daughter might have fallen victim to Ross' sweet-talking.

'I'm sorry for you, Amy. You thought he was a grouse bloke at the start. Trouble is, some men are manipulators. I never liked him in the bank and now I understand why. He's a smooth talker, all right. Don't feel bad that he took you in.'

Tracey turned to face me and rubbed her hands, gleefully. 'Now, Amy. Tell us everything that happened. From the top.'

'Everything?'

Tracey laughed. 'You're among friends and we don't embarrass easily.'

* * *

By the time we'd been to church and finished lunch on the following day, the

187

skies had clouded over. There was no blue visible, only pewter grey.

'Reckon we're in for a thunderstorm this arvo. Judging by the way them rosellas are behaving, it's going to be a real ripper.' Mr L's eyesight was clearly not that bad in the daylight.

The multi-coloured birds were wheeling around the eucalypts in a raucous frenzy. The ants were having a field-day too, busily marching to and fro. You could taste the moisture in the air.

'Hurry up, you two. Better get a wriggle on.'

Mrs L was putting a basket of fresh veg in the boot to take to Currawong. I could see chockos and squash along with butternut pumpkins.

'You ever seen a country storm, Amy?'

'No. Don't reckon they're much different to the southerly busters we have in Sydney, though.'

It was common for a few days of heatwave temperatures to end when a cold pressure system chased up from the south, bringing soaking rains and a drop of forty degrees Fahrenheit in the space of half an hour.

Mr L smiled.

'We'll have to wait and see, young lady.' He wet his finger and held it up to the freshening breeze. 'Won't have to wait long, though.'

The drive out was uneventful apart from the almost mesmerising sight of the long ears of wheat moving in languid waves as the summer breeze swept through them.

Mrs L announced from the back seat that we were having yabbies tonight. I'm afraid I showed my city ignorance once again by asking what sort of veggie they were.

There were chuckles all around me. Mr L explained. 'They're fresh water crayfish. We catch them when we go swimming in the dam down by the shearing shed.'

'Crayfish? Aren't they like lobsters?'

'I guess. Those nippers on them can

give you quite a start when you're swimming at times. Eating them is a type of revenge, I guess.'

I wasn't a big fan of prawns and such. It was yukky to clean them and, to me, there wasn't enough meat on them to be worth the trouble. Still, I wasn't a fussy eater.

Once we reached Currawong Station, we went inside the sprawling farmhouse and settled in the country kitchen built of solid wood. Joe was there, tucking into some banana cake while drinking milky tea from a mug. I guessed his huge hands couldn't handle the delicate imported china that was neatly arranged on the dresser shelves.

Naturally, Mrs L had to start off the conversation by relating my ignorance of the creatures from the bottom of the dam.

Tracey led me to a big enamel baby bath where the offending beasts were walking around in water. They were a dirty brown and those nippers would certainly cause anyone to scream if they were bitten on the toe.

'Don't tell me, Vince. You've named them all, haven't you?' I asked the burly farmer.

'Not all of them. The big one's John after . . . '

'John Wayne.'

'That one's Rock.' No need to ask; Mr Hudson.

'What about that one?' I pointed to one scurrying madly around the metal container.

'Oh,' he whispered so that no one else could hear. 'That's Ross, still searching for something he lost last night.'

At that moment, a blue heeler cattle dog bounded into the room from the lounge area. He skidded up to the bath, stuck his nose in inquisitively then yelped as a yabbie chomped on it. He flew back out of the room, yelping in pain.

'I gather that's Brigitte,' I observed wryly.

'Yeah. That's Brigitte. Our own little fruit loop.'

* * *

Later, Joe invited me to his house, which wasn't far away. He wished me to meet his family and I wanted to discuss questions I had about his life and aboriginals in general. He had two daughters at our school, both in primary classes.

Outside the sky was darkening and flashes of lightning appeared on the horizon.

'How's the first week been, Amy?'

'Hectic. I guess Vince has filled you in about most of it. No closer to finding Graham, though I'm convinced he's still alive.'

I told him about the bushranger connection.

'I heard the stories too. Starlight's Treasure. They say his ghost still guards it. Just one of those tales, Amy. If it exists, and I say if, it could be anywhere in south-western New South Wales or western Victoria. That's a mighty big area. There is one thing — my people have a story about the yellow caves that he and his men used to hole up in near some river.'

In his home, Joe and his wife, Nancy, made me most welcome. She let me taste some damper she'd made that morning. When I commented on the various paintings on the walls, Joe told me he did them. He showed me similarly decorated boomerangs and woomeras as well as a mulga wood shield hanging on the wall.

'Don't use it much these days; only at corroboree time.' I'd heard of the dance festivals.

'Could you show me how to paint like you do? I have an idea for art lessons. And can you tell me why you don't use blue paint?'

Joe pointed out there wasn't any green either.

'We have yellow, red and white from clay and black from charcoal. Also, I only have the right to paint certain scenes from our traditional tales. Things are more complicated than they seem if you wish to learn about us, Amy. Let's do some painting, then I can give you an idea.'

By the time I returned to the main house, the skies were grumbling with thunder while strobed lightning flashed storm warnings. I headed for the veranda where everyone was gathered for the show when the first giant raindrops fell. I was surprised to see Kyle there. His car must have been around the other side of the homestead.

'We need whatever rain comes, Amy. We rely on rainwater for the dams and rainwater tanks. Haven't had a decent downpour since October.'

I saw Vince had emptied the rain gauge of dust, preparing to make an accurate reading for the farm records.

And so we stood, or sat on the cane chairs, watching. Within seconds, the heavens opened, drumming on the corrugated tin roof above us like some demented musician. The din was incredible but it was nothing compared to the virtual solid waterfall that crashed onto the grass and soil.

We couldn't see more than five feet from the house. The silvery wall was everywhere around us. Tracey switched on the lights above us even though dusk would be another three hours.

'All right. I'm impressed,' I shouted into the ear of Mr L.

'Thought you might be,' he shouted back.

After twenty minutes it stopped, just like that. The sun peeked through widening spaces in the clouds.

'Just over an inch. More to come, apparently,' Vince announced while that daft dog of theirs chased his tail through the puddles.

'Why are you here, Senior Constable?' I asked Kyle. 'And in civvies. Will wonders never cease?'

'I'm here for the same reason as you, Miss Shaw. To enjoy a meal in good company . . . and to catch up on your investigations.'

'Mine? I'm hardly a detective.'

'Maybe not. I have noticed something about you that you may not realise that you have.'

'And what's that, pray tell? A lovely disposition, beautiful hair, engaging smile?' I mentally kicked myself. Flirting with a married man? Damn it. Ross had screwed up my emotions something awful. 'Sorry. Ignore that, Kyle. I'm as daft as Brigitte these days.'

'I was going to say you have that special skill to see the big picture. I believe it's called lateral thinking — searching outside the conventional square. Working out that Graham may have been snatched by car, for instance.'

'I simply have ideas. I make mistakes, more than my share.' Thinking of Ross, I blurted, 'I'm not as good a judge of character as I thought.' I wasn't going to tell anyone else about what Ross had tried to do last night. As Gail had said, females' reputations were very tenuous in the small-town mentality. 'Anyway, why haven't you brought Tuesday with you today?'

Kyle appeared surprised at that question.

'Why would I? She'd probably go walkabout and we'd spend ages searching for her.'

'Go walkabout?'

Then it hit me. At that moment I felt dumber than Brigitte, plus all the galahs and wombats in the whole of Australia put together.

'Tuesday's not your wife, then?'

'Wife? Me?' He burst out into the biggest laugh possible. I felt two inches tall.

'You told me that I might come for a meal with you and Tuesday after we figured out the thermite.' I was in defensive mode.

'Tuesday's my cat, Amy. She was born here on Currawong.' I banged my head against a veranda post. 'Hence the name, Tuesday. Vince up to his tricks. Named after Tuesday Weld.'

Then I recalled Mrs L and her hints for us to get together. She'd probably invited Kyle today.

Tracey opened the screen door.

'What's the big joke, Kyle?'

'Don't you dare — ' I began but I was too late. My day was going from bad to disastrous.

'Amy here thought I was married . . . to Tuesday.'

Tracey sniggered before seeing my pleading expression. Other faces appeared.

'What's happening?' Mrs L asked.

Ignoring my frantic silent pleas, Tracey blabbed it out for everyone. The cat was literally out of the bag. How mortifying. I cringed until I felt Kyle's arms encircle me in a reassuring Daddy hug.

'I'm sorry, Amy. It was so . . . unbelievable, that's all,' he said in his most comforting voice.

Tracey chirped in.

'Yeah. The idea that anyone intelligent would possibly marry you, Kyle. Un . . . believable.'

That broke the tension as Kyle vainly protested. Finally I joined in the light-hearted ribbing. So what if I was a proper goose? I had my new friends and I was happy.

★   ★   ★

Our yabbie dinner was a treat. By agreement the grand-daddy of all the yabbies, John Wayne, was given to me. Mr L summed it up.

'After that Kyle marriage fiasco, you need all the brain food you can manage, Amy.'

Kyle and I were given the jobs of washing and drying up.

'I can understand why I'm doing this — but why you, Kyle? You didn't screw anything up.'

'Maybe I should have changed Tuesday's name to something like Dog or Mouse or Fluffywuggles. At least then, no one would consider we were man and wife.'

I put some more Sunlight into the hot water, grateful for the gloves I had on.

'I've been thinking about us, Kyle.'

'Us? There is no 'us'.'

'Don't you like me at all?'

'I 'spose. You're bright and funny.'

'Actually, I mean *like* like.'

'Oh. *Like* like? I hadn't thought about it much. You're a lot younger than me.'

'Only six years.'

This wasn't going very well.

Anyway, it should be the guy's job to chase the girl. Trouble was, I hated conventions like that. I remembered all those school dances waiting on the girl's side of the room for a boy to ask me to dance. Why couldn't it be the other way around? So one night I'd marched across no-man's land and asked some lanky guy to dance with me.

He'd looked like a terrified rabbit in

a car's headlights before stammering 'No.'

It hadn't put me off. Next time I'd been more selective with my victim. He'd been making goo-goo eyes at me for fifteen minutes. He said Yes.

It only lasted one dance, though. His breath would have sunk the Bismark, no worries.

Kyle didn't ask how I'd learned his age. I was grateful for that.

'I thought you fancied that bloke from the City and Country Bank. Heard you two went out.'

'His name's Ross and I don't fancy him any more. Suffice to say, I tossed his car keys in the scrub. He's probably still looking for them.'

'Anything I should know about as a policeman?'

'Naw. His word against mine. You should chat to the other local girls about him, though.'

He was drying the defenceless plate so much, I thought he'd clean the pattern right off it.

'This Ross fella. Did he hurt you? Maybe you should see the doc.'

It was my turn to scoff.

'Kyle, I've seen the doc just about every day since I arrived in Gurawang. Poor bloke, losing his wife like that. I gather she was a nice person. How did she die? A car accident?'

'Yeah. Real shame. She went off the road on the West Burumba Road, up near Brolga Ridge. Not my patch. Another copper dealt with it and broke the news to Doc MacAlister. I must have been busy at the time.'

West Burumba? That was out past Currawong Station. There had been road signs on the drive to Vince and Tracey's. My mind suddenly went from lazy Sunday night mode to full alertness.

Mrs L wandered into the kitchen to start brewing tea for us all.

'Mrs L? Sorry to bother you. What date did the doctor's wife get killed?'

'Oh, now you're asking, Amy. The date? Wait — I think it was the same day young Graham disappeared. Early afternoon.'

I shot a look at Kyle.

'Are you thinking what I'm thinking?' I asked.

We all went back into the lounge room, the shocking truth scaring the hell out of me. I needed to check with the others. Was I jumping to a conclusion that was simply too incredible?

'I'm sorry to spoil the party, everyone,' I said anxiously, scanning the room. Vince's daughter was in bed. Good. I didn't want to upset her.

'What's on your mind, Amy?'

'We've only now realised that Morag MacAlister died on the same day as Graham went missing. What I'm wondering is if there's a connection.'

'Go on, Amy.' It was Tracey.

'Suppose Mrs MacAlister was driving by the creek and saw Graham being bundled into a car. What would she do?'

Kyle was keeping a low profile. I

decided he was seeing my approach to the situation.

'Keep driving? Go for help?'

'And what would the kidnappers do once they realised they'd been seen?'

'Chase her, of course. Try to stop her.' Mr L spoke for everyone.

'If they couldn't make her stop?'

There was silence. Mrs L put her clenched hand to her mouth before stating in a clear, sombre voice. 'Force her off the road, ideally down some ravine where she'd have no chance of survival.' We all took deep breaths, each of us upset.

Kyle took over. 'This means that Graham's kidnappers have already killed. I'm afraid I have to leave now, get back to the station. I'll contact my colleague Rob Naylor. He was the copper who dealt with the crash. I need to let my district chief know too. My God. The murder of someone we all knew . . . and respected.' I saw a tear in his eye.

'I think we'd better head off now too,

Amy,' murmured Mrs L. 'This is all so very upsetting.'

Mr L clasped his hands together. 'Let's pray for little Graham. Wherever he is and whatever he's doing for that monster, let us pray that he, at least, is still alive.'

'Dear God . . . '

★　★　★

The drive back home was quiet. I guess we were all lost in our own thoughts, and that the realisation that Morag MacAlister might have been murdered must have been far more personal to the Levinsons. We agreed to say nothing to the doc at this stage. It was only speculation.

As we rounded the corner of Kookaburra Road, I was surprised to see a car parked on the road rather than in the drive like our other neighbours. It was in the shadows as the last of the street lighting finished near the Levinsons' home.

I pulled into the drive and got out to open the garage door. A dark-clad figure darted from the side of the garage, startling us. He wore a mask.

'Watch out, Amy!' Mrs L called. The shadow tried to bypass me but I put my foot out to trip him. He crashed onto the concrete drive, screaming in pain. I moved up behind to hold him down.

He kicked me in the left shin causing me to stagger. Before I could recover, the intruder was on his feet, legging it for the parked car. I watched as it started off. In seconds he was gone.

'You all right, Amy?' Mrs L asked worriedly.

'Yeah. More bruises to add to my collection.'

Mr L arrived with the car torch, shining it on the ground. Dark splodges of blood showed that I hurt him. Good. I was tired of being Miss Black and Blue, 1970.

'What was he doing here?' Mrs L asked.

'No idea, but I recognise that car.

Circular rear light cluster. A Cortina Mark 1. Soon I'll track him down. You two go inside after I check around.'

'A cup of tea for everyone? And maybe something a little stronger,' said Mrs L.

10

Fortunately the masked man hadn't broken in. He had however left another note.

At this rate, I'd soon have a book full of menacing words from my local 'admirers'. I didn't mention it to the Levinsons.

Mrs L's 'something stronger' was brandy. She insisted it was a medicine for special occasions yet I was aware of the taste from one time with my dad. I didn't like it at the time, but when mixed with tea that night, it hit the spot.

The note was more concise this time. *Your days are numbered, Amy Shaw.* The cut-out letters had a photo of a handgun pasted underneath them.

The following day at school, a number of students commented on my bruised leg.

'It was a pig,' I told them nonchalantly.

'If a pig had kicked my mum like that, Miss, he'd be sausages by tea time,' one boy told me.

I did ask my classes if anyone was aware of a Cortina owner in the town. Most didn't have the faintest what a Cortina looked like.

During afternoon art class, I introduced the girls to aboriginal art styles. I showed them examples as well as explaining the colour palette. Then we drew boomerangs on thick cardboard before cutting them out. We used the ends of match sticks to apply individual dots describing scenes or animals like kangaroos. Finally I showed them one of Joe's exquisitely painted boomerangs that we went out into the playground to throw. My training had been basic, but it did manage to turn in mid-flight before landing fifty feet away.

I regarded the lesson as a success when one of the younger girls admired her own dotted masterpiece. 'Miss, I guess I can draw after all.'

'I guess you can, Josie. Lovely emu there.'

★ ★ ★

After school, Colin dropped in to see how I was.

'As you're on probation, I need to view some of your lessons, Amy. I was thinking Year Two science tomorrow. Could I see your lesson plans?'

I showed him.

'Introduction to geology? Rocks and different types? Oh, and a volcano? Sounds interesting. I'm looking forward to it. One other thing — we have the first P and C meeting of the year tomorrow. You'd be most welcome to come along to meet the parents. Eight o'clock in the library.'

'Will Peter Gilmore be there?'

'He's the president so yes, he'll be there.'

'Not looking forward to that, Colin. I

210

get the feeling he'll want to have a go at me.'

'I'll be there too, as well as the Robinsons and Tracey Levinson. Don't worry about Peter.'

The trouble was, I did. I hardly had any sleep that night and when I did drop off, I had nightmares about being chased around the playground by Mr Gilmore, his trained toupee snapping at my heels.

* * *

Tuesday began with assembly as per normal. We were in for another day of heavy showers apparently. Colin came into the lab along with Year Two, taking a seat up the back. It was his task to evaluate me and decide if I'd be appointed as a fully-qualified teacher. No pressure, then.

I chose to begin with a demonstration of a volcanic eruption ... on a small scale, of course. I piled up some ammonium dichromate in front of the students who were gathered at a safe distance. I had a pupil standing by with a fire extinguisher, though I was certain we'd not need it. I then lit it with a taper.

'Nothing's happening, Miss.'

'Oh rats,' I said, turning away, feigning disappointment. Some pupils moaned.

'Wait. It's . . . it's smoking.'

We looked back as the orange crystals changed to black, expanding as they did so. Then sparks cascaded everywhere from the cone top just like a firework. The volcano grew and grew and grew until a smoking mass of black was left.

'Wow,' a few said in awe.

I then pointed to a group of ten rocks on the front bench, explaining the importance of knowing about rocks for building and agriculture as examples. I taught them about the three groups; igneous, sedimentary and metamorphic.

'A lot of igneous rocks are formed by volcanoes erupting all across the world over millions of years. There weren't any near here. Volcanoes produce rocks like basalt. I have some here to show you but unfortunately I've lost the labels. Is this basalt?' I picked up some sandstone.

There was a moment of silence before a very quiet voice said. 'That's sandstone, Miss. It's all around here and it's sedimentary, not igneous. We use it to make chimneys in our houses.'

'You sure, Stanley? It looks like basalt to me.'

'No, Miss. This one's basalt,' he told the class, holding a black-grey rock up for us all to see. 'And this one here is marble. It's metamorphic. There's some on the bench in the bank.'

The following twenty minutes went quickly as I guided Stanley to do my lesson for me. At the end the class gave him a cheer for a great job.

As the bell rang and the class left for their next lesson, Colin came up, looking displeased.

'A great start with your volcanic

demonstration, Amy, but I have to say I was very disappointed in your obvious lack of preparation. If it hadn't been for Stanley helping you out, well, the lesson would have been a disaster. I've never seen Stanley talk so much in all my years here. He was a much more confident . . . ' At that point Colin stared at me as the truth hit him. 'You sneaky little . . . All right, Miss Shaw. I'm impressed. I assume you'll come clean tomorrow about your little charade? Can't do with the kids thinking you don't understand what you're supposed to be teaching.'

'I'm reasonably certain most of the class worked that out already and were simply playing along for Stanley's sake. They like him, though he's been too shy to realise that. I wouldn't be surprised to see Laura sitting with him at lunchtime today.' I'd noticed the way she was watching him do his rock lecture.

'Laura and Stanley? What a combination.'

We both signed off on his lesson evaluation. I was well pleased with the final comment:

No suggestions for improvement required.

If only I could be so confident about tonight's P and C meeting.

★ ★ ★

At three o'clock, I decided to go to the bank. My finances were lower than I wanted and Ross had assured me the cheque I'd deposited would be cleared. I'd paid extra for that service. Of course, meeting Ross again was right up there with having all my teeth extracted without anaesthetic. There was only one teller at that bank and it was him.

As I hurried down the main street, I was amazed to see a certain Cortina parked outside the bank so I walked even faster. The driver was chatting to another man on the opposite side of the car. The pedestrian was Ross.

Doreen came out of the general

store, greeting me warmly. I saw Ross rush back into the bank.

'Sorry, Doreen. In a hurry to go to the bank before it closes. One thing — that bloke driving the Cortina? Do you recognise him?'

'Not sure of his name. Sleazy fellow. Makes my skin crawl. He doesn't come into town often.'

'Anything more?'

'Oh yeah. He rents a place out of town with that young bank bloke and a Yank.'

'What the . . . Sorry, Doreen. Have to run. I'll catch up with you tomorrow. Promise.'

I couldn't believe it. That so-and-so Ross had set me up big time. At the dance, he'd clearly sent in his fish-faced best mate to soften me up, make a pretence of a rescue and stupid-headed Amy became putty in his scheming, conniving hands. Lord, how gullible was I?

I decided to tell Kyle later. It looked like Fish-face was the bloke who gave me those nasty notes. Probably he was involved in the kidnap too. I checked my watch. Ten past three. Time to get my money out first.

There were a few people in the bank impatient to do their own transactions. Gail, the young woman who'd warned me about Ross, was there with an older lady, presumably her mum.

I whispered to Gail as I passed, 'Thanks for telling me about him. Sadly I've made Ross an enemy for life. I stranded him in the bush on Saturday night. Wish me luck.'

Deciding to treat him as impersonally as possible, I pushed my bank book across with a signed withdrawal slip, making sure I didn't let him intimidate me.

He glared at me, glanced at my pass book and said, 'Your cheque hasn't cleared yet. Next.'

I was fuming. The lying toe-rag. Deciding to step aside for the next customer, I chose another tack. It was clear Ross wasn't prepared to help.

I called across to the manager who was doing whatever bank managers do. In this case, it appeared to be nothing.

'The teller will attend to you, madam,' was his curt response. He put his glasses on, resuming doing nothing. It seemed a little feminine subterfuge was required.

'I'm so sorry, but I really need the advice of an older, more experienced man and you appear to be much more knowledgeable than that . . . child on the teller booth. Please?'

He paused, uncertain what to do. Despite every cell of my body protesting at the sheer indignity of it all, I batted my eyelashes.

I was aware that I was the centre of attention in the bank by this point. Even randy Ross was watching the drama unfold.

Mr Manager put on his best smiley face.

'How may I assist you, young lady?'

I showed him my book and the receipt for rapid clearance. 'Your Mr

Wilkinson told me my pay cheque hasn't cleared. I don't believe him.'

'I'm sure he wouldn't lie . . . Wait. Miss Shaw, isn't it? I saw your details earlier. Yes, it has cleared. I must apologise for the slight error. Mr Wilkinson will give you your money.'

'No. Not him. You do it.' I was adamant.

'This is highly irregular. May I ask why?' he said in a low voice.

I saw Gail speaking to her mother and other women. Two farmer types moved to listen in.

'I don't trust him. He deliberately lied to me just now.' I wasn't whispering. 'In addition, he tried to assault me the other night.'

'The bank is hardly responsible for what our employees do on their free time . . . '

Gail's mother stepped forward.

'He did the same to my daughter. Left her stranded out in the scrub at night.'

I smiled delightedly at Gail. She'd

found the courage to tell others.

'As I said, it's nothing to do with our bank . . . '

'Perhaps Gail's grandfather might see it differently,' Gail's mother said.

'And who's that?'

'Jeremy Holland. Your largest investor.'

Mr Manager's face paled. He went over to take five ten-dollar notes from Ross' till, then shoved my withdrawal slip into the drawer. I heard one of the blokes talking to the small group.

'My daughter hasn't been the same since he took her to the movies. You don't think . . . ?'

Gathering my money I headed for the door, my legs feeling as soft as jelly. That confrontation had totally drained me.

Ross wasn't finished, though.

'You bitch. You ugly, skinny bitch. It took me seven hours to find my keys. Seven hours.'

It was an invective which didn't go unnoticed by the manager.

'Mr Wilkinson! Hold your tongue.'

Ross lifted a chair and flung it at his boss, who narrowly avoided being struck. Ross then strode out from behind the marble counter, grabbing my arm and raising his fist. I cowered, expecting the worst, but two burly men stepped in to release me, sending Ross sprawling on the polished floor.

'You leave him to us, Miss Shaw. You've done your share,' one of them said, tipping his hat. 'This smarmy scum won't bother you or any of our girls no more.'

I exited rather more quickly than a lady should. What would the headlines be on this week's newspaper? *School Teacher Causes Riot in Bank?* I felt like a walking disaster area. All I wanted to do was go home and curl up on the bed.

I should have brought my teddy with me from Sydney, despite being told off for being such a baby with it. There were times when even a grown woman needed a teddy to cuddle and this arvo was definitely one of them.

Worse still, my day from hell was not yet over. There was the P and C with grumpy Gilmore tonight. Life was not meant to be easy.

A car pulled up suddenly right next to me. I hoped it wasn't a Cortina.

'Need a drink?' It was a smiling Judith. 'I noticed the fracas outside the bank. Was that anything to do with you?'

'A . . . a little,' I stammered with a wan smile, before bursting into tears. Judith stepped out to hold me before leading me to the passenger side.

'Buckle up, kiddo. Let's go to my place. You can have dinner tonight with me and Colin. I'll tell Mrs Levinson where you are.'

* * *

Judith was a life-saver. It took a while for me to open up about Ross. Alice, one of the other teachers, dropped by, not realising I was there. She explained the gossip was that things had become quite heated after I'd left the bank.

The bank manager had tried to call the police for assistance. By the time Kyle had returned from erecting flood warnings on roads, Ross had gone to his rental place, packed and left Gurawang, vowing never to return. Other young ladies had come forward to complain to the police. More upsetting for the bank manager than losing his only employee, had been the realisation that Ross had somehow made off with the contents of the tills. Alice described the manager being as sick as a dead chook at a barbie.

I spoke to Kyle on the phone about Cortina Man. It came as no surprise to learn that he and Ross were living in the same shack as the American railway guy. There was a connection there, but not the connection to Graham we were searching for. None of the three had a moustache, so none of them stole the gelignite or blew up the wagon.

Kyle said he'd bring Cortina Man in

for questioning and probably arrest him for dangerous driving the night of the dance. He asked if I'd press charges. I said I would, if only to wipe the grin off that fishy face of his.

At seven-thirty Judith, Colin and I walked across to open up the school library. Tracey and Vince arrived moments later with sausage rolls, sarnies and cakes for after. I mentally earmarked a pink lammie for yours truly. Peter Gilmore arrived at five to, his eldest daughter, Rhonda, by his side.

I always find the rigmarole of formal meetings boring; apologies for absence, minutes of the last meeting and so on. It was one of those necessary evils of grown-up life, I guessed.

Colin introduced me to the twenty or so parents who were there. Doreen was one of them. I could see that Peter Gilmore was eager to move things along. He asked to move to General Business before any of the tabled items on the agenda.

Judith squeezed my hand, sensing my apprehension. Peter Gilmore and his wig stood up to address the meeting.

'As a parent myself, I have to say I'm very disappointed in the actions of our latest import from the Big Smoke.'

'Here it comes,' I muttered to myself. What was it to be; the newspaper article about me rescuing Sharon? My going to the pictures with a man? Maybe even the incident at the bank?

'Yesterday Miss Shaw took it upon herself to teach her art class about aboriginal painting and had them paint scenes on card boomerangs in the same way our more primitive native inhabitants do. Are you going to deny it, Miss Shaw?'

I wasn't prepared for that. Of all the things . . .

'No — I certainly won't deny it, Mr Gilmore.'

'Why did you do this?' he demanded.

I took a deep breath to compose myself.

'Art isn't only about Rome, Greece

or Egypt. We study all cultures including Renaissance Europe, China and modern American artists such as Andy Warhol. Native Australian art has existed longer than any of those cultures.'

'And do you approve of this, Headmaster?'

Great. Now he was putting Colin on the spot.

'Wholeheartedly, Mr Gilmore. I'm distributing copies of the approved art syllabus for all New South Wales schools. Item 21.5 clearly encourages Miss Shaw's initiative by extolling the virtues of teaching aboriginal artistic skills.'

I hadn't realised that. It simply seemed like a good idea to me at the time. I wasn't aware that it was actually in the syllabus.

Peter Gilmore glanced at the document.

'I see. I apologise, then.'

Judith nudged me.

'Colin got wind of his complaint. We

weren't going to throw you to the dogs, kiddo.'

Gilmore wasn't finished, though.

'Miss Shaw does have other undesirable personal qualities. Most of you have heard that our highly respected bank clerk, Mr Ross Wilkinson, has left town. Miss Shaw's slanderous and malicious gossip led to this. Ross was an upright member of our community. I met him a number of times in my shop and the bank.

'He asked my permission to take my daughter, Rhonda, out the Saturday before last. Their future was promising until Amy Shaw threw herself at Ross, who succumbed to her harlot ways. He left my Rhonda, breaking her heart. That — ' He pointed a finger. 'That is the loose sort of woman we mistakenly welcomed into our hearts.'

I was on my feet in an instant. 'What?'

I felt Colin's hand on my shoulder.

'Peter. That is well out of ord — '

'Stop it. Stop It, everyone.' It was

Rhonda, screaming at the top of her voice. 'Dad. Ross was horrible. Evil and horrible. He . . . he forced me . . . to do sex with him.'

She broke down in tears, rushing out of the library door. Judith ran after her while Peter stood in shocked silence, his shoulders slumped.

'My princess. He hurt my princess. How could I have let him?'

He was about to follow them until Colin laid a restraining hand on Peter's shoulder.

'Not yet, Peter. Give Judith a few minutes with her. Come into my office.' He faced the rest of us. 'I'm sorry, ladies and gentlemen. I suggest we postpone the meeting for tonight. Please, enjoy the refreshments before you go. Have a chat with Amy if you wish. She can use all of your support.'

Gail's mother was the first to come over to me.

'I wanted to thank you personally. Seems that Ross guy had warned the girls to be quiet. If it hadn't been for you in the bank, standing up to him, I doubt Gail would have told me the full story. And now there's Rhonda. Peter has doted on his daughters ever since his wife left.'

Others came over to talk to us. After fifteen minutes or so, Colin returned with Judith. They appeared shattered and sad.

'Peter?' I said.

'He's taken Rhonda home. I think they'll be OK. Judith has offered to help with counselling. She's had training with rape cases.'

'I feel so upset for them both. Though I admit I didn't like Peter, I wouldn't wish that on any father . . . or Rhonda.'

'We phoned Kyle. He's been trying to track Ross down for hours. No luck.'

Outside it was already dark. The group were going their separate ways as Vince and Tracey packed the food leftovers away. Tracey came over, holding a paper plate with a lamington on it.

'I heard you're partial to them.' She smiled.

'Ah, thanks — but not now. I don't feel like it.'

'I'll wrap it up for later, Amy. Sometimes when the world is collapsing all around us, one little cake can give us the strength to carry on.'

I nodded, certain she was right. Things were happening with increased speed. I had a feeling a breakthrough to find Doreen's son was close. I prayed we wouldn't be too late.

'I'll drive you home, Amy,' Judith offered. 'Just started raining again. Bucketing down and looks like it's set in for the night.'

11

It was pouring on Wednesday too; unrelenting, Biblical-deluge torrents of rain. A number of roads around Gurawang were impassable and at least twenty kids hadn't been able to get in.

I stared out of the windows of the staff room, awash with water.

'So much for static electricity experiments,' I told Alice, the English teacher. 'Any ideas?'

'Maybe you need some magic? Mr Knovak was a chemistry teacher originally. He used to show us stuff in the staff room that looked like magic but was just tricks with chemicals. He never bothered with the kids, though. He preferred to have them read text books than to teach the fun stuff.'

I thought. There were a few reactions our college tutor had given us; flash powder, another volcano with Condy's crystals and glycerine? Perhaps if I were to dress up with a magician's hat and use a wand? I'd ask the students to observe and tell me how I might do my tricks.

It finished up being a good lesson. I completed my stage performance with a colour change experiment. Two of my student helpers each held up a test tube of water; at least the liquid appeared to be water. When I waved my wand and spoke a spell, the helpers poured the liquid from one test tube into the other. The contents turned bright yellow. That brought a few wows.

I held up the yellow vial of lead iodide formed from the precipitation reaction.

'So, was it real magic?'

'I don't think it was only water, Miss.'

'Did I say it was water? Or did you make an assumption?' Then I explained the chemistry.

'I guess you believe what you want to believe,' said Laura, summing up. I didn't realise that her words would help me make the breakthrough about Graham being seized.

★ ★ ★

Lunchtime was a washout. I was on duty while the kids ate and played a little under cover in the playground. It was a shame because I loved to see them run around. My own days of excessive energy were gone. These days, I took pleasure in my sports yet I enjoyed taking a rest also.

As I predicted, Stanley was with Laura, both examining the rocks he'd brought to school. Laura ran over to me as I approached them.

'Look, Miss. It's gold.' She put the chunk into my open hand. I appraised its weight.

'Certainly feels like gold, Laura. A piece this large would be worth a lot.' We walked to where she and Stanley had been sitting.

'See you later, Stanley,' she said,

before happily skipping off. I returned the sample to him.

'Impressive, Stanley. I assume it's iron pyrites? Fool's Gold. Certainly fooled me.'

'No — it's proper gold, Miss. Just under a pound in weight.'

'That would be a great deal of money if you sold it. Your parents would appreciate it. Last time I looked, gold was over thirty dollars a troy ounce. Why are you so certain?'

'I read up about it. If you put some drops of nitric acid on a scratched bit and nothing happens, then it's probably pure gold.'

Geology wasn't my forte but that sounded right. Gold was unreactive, which is why it can be found as pure rather than in a compound like copper oxide or copper carbonate.

'Where did you get it? No, that's rude of me. I mean, did someone give it to you?'

'Graham did. Said he found it with this limestone.' He showed me the creamish rock found in places like Jenolan Caves near Lithgow.

Gold nuggets in limestone? I didn't have any idea. Nevertheless this prompted me to think again about the reason Graham may have been snatched. What if he or his grandfather knew where there was some gold?

★   ★   ★

After school, I decided to visit Doreen at the Railway Hotel. It had ceased raining for the moment, but it was a pain walking around all the puddles on the mud footpath. A car was a priority.

The milk-bar was on the way. I decided to call in.

'G'day, Amy. Got a special treat here. Tra-la. Banana syrup — just for you.' Beryl held up the bottle and I beamed. Civilisation had arrived in Gurawang!

'Heard about you and that Ross bloke down at the bank. Sounded like a right ding-dong. Can't say I liked the bloke, though I reckon you did for a time. Weird bloke, with them jellies he wanted.'

I waited as she made up my drink. Two scoops of ice-cream, too — it was heaven. I was almost finished slurping the last few drops when her description of Ross registered.

'Beryl. What about the jellies?'

'Him. No one ever buys mandarin flavour except Doreen for that son of hers . . . the one on the posters, you know.'

Luckily I'd already paid. I was out of there like a possum up a gum tree, sprinting back to the school. I almost slipped twice and was panting for breath by the time I reached Colin's office. I burst in without knocking.

'Colin . . . ' I had my hands on my knees as I struggled for breath. 'Can . . . I have . . . a special meeting, in my lab? Half an hour?'

'Come in, Amy.' Colin laughed. 'You look a right mess.' I hadn't lifted my gaze from the floor. As I did so, I realised how right he was. I had mud splattered on my shoes, socks, even on my dress. I straightened up sheepishly. Not very lady-like. Then I saw Peter Gilmore.

'Sorry. Didn't realise you had company.' I began to back out.

'Wait up, Amy. I came here to talk to you also. To apologise for every nasty thing I've said.'

Surprised, I looked at Peter and wiped a hand across my cheek. He seemed genuinely contrite.

'Ahem.' Colin motioned at my face. I peeked in a mirror on the wall. Mud splodges everywhere.

'I must seem a proper scuff bunny, but what I found out about Graham couldn't wait. I need to have a big meeting with everyone involved. Hopefully we'll solve this jigsaw between us.'

'No worries, Amy. Tell me who you want there and I'll phone them now,' Colin suggested. 'Meanwhile, I suggest you clean yourself up. Judith's at home, she'll have a dress to fit you.'

'Could I come to your get-together,

too?' enquired Peter. 'I'd like to assist if I can. I might know things no one else is aware of.'

'Sure. You'd be welcome. How's Rhonda?'

'Not good. She's with her aunt now. It . . . it was a difficult conversation. I had no idea I was that unapproachable — or that Ross was that devious. If it hadn't been for you confronting him, heaven knows how many others he would have preyed on. To think I actually liked that so-and-so . . . '

I liked this new side of Peter. I could only imagine how he'd felt once he'd discovered Rhonda had been even more of a victim than the rest of us girls. Things like that change your priorities quickly and it seemed Peter now realised it was time to encourage support from the people around him.

'He hoodwinked me too, Peter. Gail was the one who warned me. I pray that the cops catch up with him, for robbing the tills if nothing else.'

'You haven't heard? The auditors were in today. Ross made off with a lot more than that. Apparently that sports car of his was 'financed' by the local business community including me. We'll get all our money back, of course. The bank has promised us that. Some very red faces and, I strongly suspect, a new manager will be appointed. Ross made fools of us all.'

★ ★ ★

By the time I'd washed and changed, we had a classroom of budding detectives. I should have thought of doing this before, but I'd been distracted by the events of my own life, both Ross and Peter contributing to that in their own ways.

I'd reasoned that we all had pieces of the jigsaw puzzle that covered Graham's kidnapping, the explosion and more. By putting everyone together, I was confident we could make the breakthrough as to the reason he'd been taken plus where he might now be.

Peter entered my classroom last. I could sense Mrs L's hostility from feet away.

'What's he doing here?' she demanded.

I was about to defend him. However Peter, ever the leader, spoke first.

'I'm here because my daughter was assaulted by Ross Wilkinson, a man I trusted and who may be linked to Graham's disappearance. Even if he isn't, I'll help in anyway I can. I realise I've treated some of you badly, professionally and personally. That includes Miss Shaw. I've been wrong about a lot of things but I'm going to try and put things right. But I won't stay if you don't want me to.'

Mrs Levinson answered more calmly.

'If you can give us some clues to solve this dreadful mystery, you're welcome, Mr Gilmore. You can sit next to me.'

'Thanks. And please, call me Peter.'

We had our group together. It was a mixture, all right. Standing with me at the front was Kyle. The Levinsons, senior and junior, were there along with Peter Gilmore, Doreen Robinson, Colin with Judith Anderson and finally Barbara, the Reverend's wife.

'Thanks for coming, everyone,' said Doreen. 'It's been almost six weeks since my precious boy went missing. The Senior Constable, tells me it appears to be a kidnap. And now he and Amy have accumulated some more information.'

She sat down and I took over.

'I'm going to summarise what we've found or believe is important. Please don't let's get sidetracked by shock at what we tell you. If you have something to add, feel free. I think the secret to sorting this out lies in sharing facts that some of us know but may not understand the importance of.'

I started chalking on the blackboard. Mr L might struggle to read so I intended to repeat it.

Kyle stepped up.

'I'll write, Amy. You talk and use that mind of yours to look for connections we've all missed.'

I nodded. It made sense.

'Graham vanished at around two o'clock on the nineteenth of December. Kyle found a hankie soaked in chloroform at the creek. Doctor MacAlister's wife, Morag, died at about two-forty in a car accident at Brolga Ridge. We believe she was murdered because she saw what happened and was being chased by someone we call Moriarty and perhaps one other.'

There was an undercurrent of incredulity within the room. Only a few of us knew about the murder.

Kyle spoke up. 'I've called my colleague who dealt with the crash. He re-checked the car wreck. It was pushed off the road by another car. A red one, based on the scratches.'

'Ross had a red Holden; a Torana. He purchased that little sports car of his just over a month ago.' It was Peter who added that.

'Great. That's the type of information we need. Thanks, Peter.' Kyle made a note on the board, *Hit by Ross' car?* next to *Doc's wife killed*.

'Ross might be involved. That's backed up by Ross buying multiple packets of mandarin jelly from Beryl at the milk-bar. Mandarin is — '

'The only flavour that Graham eats,' Doreen blurted out. 'That means he might be alive. So Ross bought them to keep him happy?'

'We hope so, Doreen.' Kyle wrote *buys jelly* next to *Ross*.

'But why take my son? I can't work it out.'

Hesitantly I held up Stanley's golden nugget.

'Is that . . . ?'

'Gold. Apparently. Graham gave it to another student.'

'Stanley?' Colin guessed. I nodded.

'But where would a nine-year-old boy find gold?' Tracey asked.

I turned to Doreen. She was struggling to digest all of this.

'Graham's grandfather was a prospector. He and Graham would spend the weekends fossicking up near Dad's shack in the Outback.'

'Was?'

'He died in late November.' She looked around at the faces watching her.

Kyle was first to ask. 'How did he die, Doreen?'

'Cyanide poisoning. He used the stuff to help extract gold from its impurities. Used it for years. I guess it simply caught up with him.'

It was Judith who spoke up now.

'I used to be a nurse. One thing I remember is that no Aussie miner has ever died from cyanide poisoning. They use minute amounts and any experienced prospector would be aware of the risks. Didn't anyone query it? Doctor? Police?'

'Yes. They did. But then Graham disappeared and . . . oh, no. You're

suggesting he might have been murdered too? Jimmy's dad? Why?'

'The gold?' Mrs Levinson said.
'Maybe he was killed because he
wouldn't disclose where he'd discovered it. Then they grabbed Graham
instead to force him to help them steal
it.'

'Them? I thought it was Ross acting
alone?' Peter asked.

Kyle's turn. 'No. There's at least one
more. Lots of clues about him. Amy
saw the bomber; he had a moustache.
He made thermite to steal gelignite
from the rail van he blew up, had access
to chloroform to subdue Graham,
maybe cyanide too. Anything else?' He
turned to me as he added the facts
about Moriarty to the board.

'We think he might have access to a
surgery, chemist or hospital although
we've checked if any of them had
missing chemicals. No joy.'

Mr L called out. 'That note he sent
to threaten you, Amy — it had
American spelling in it.'

'That's too much of a coincidence.' Colin was on his feet. 'Amy's predecessor Charles Knovak called himself Chuck. He grew up in America.'

Kyle was puzzled, as were Peter and Vince Levinson.

'You must be wrong, Colin. He didn't talk with a Yank accent. We all met him a few times.'

'He spoke like an Aussie but he spelled like a Yank. Caused all sorts of problems clashing with our English teacher.'

I tried to take in the newest revelation.

'He'd have access to the chemicals here, but the chloroform bottles are full. Hold on — '

My mind was trying to process conflicting information. Then I recalled the conversation after my 'magic' class earlier. What had Laura said about the clear liquid seeming like water? *I guess you believe what you want to believe.*

'Excuse me a moment. Judith, could

you grab the stock book and come with me, please?'

As Kyle continued to elaborate about the thermite and the nasty threatening notes to me, Judith and I went into the store room.

'Wake me up if I faint,' I told her, unscrewing the dark glass chloroform bottle. I wafted my open hand across the top. Nothing. I did it again then took a deep sniff from the bottle.

'The sneaky little . . . ' I told Judith. 'He's replaced the chloroform, probably with water. I never checked — the bottle was full.'

'You know what this means? He could have switched or stolen dozens of these chemicals.'

'Could I get you to check numbers on these?'

'Sure, kiddo.'

I scribbled a list before returning to the classroom. Kyle stopped talking as I explained.

'It looks as if Knovak covered his tracks. Put water in the chloroform bottle. Probably took other chemicals too. The stuff to make thermite, for example. But how?'

Colin answered that. 'When he left suddenly, he never returned the lab keys. And Judith and I were away for a few weeks in the school hols. Maybe he snuck back then?'

'Do you have a photo of him, Colin?' Kyle asked. 'I'll need it to pass onto my boss in Leeton. I've already sent a photo of Ross by that new Magnafax Telecopier in the police station.'

I examined the chalkboard. Kyle had included a big question mark behind Graham's name.

'We still have no idea where he might be or why they still need him,' I admitted.

It was Barbara who broke the depressive silence. 'Captain Starlight?'

I'd almost forgotten the connection. My brain was swirling with all of this new information and the implications. Barbara stood up to address us.

'As I told Judith and Amy, he actually

existed. His real name was Lion Judah O'Lachlan. The story is that he cached his stolen loot in caves out west. Gold nuggets, sovereigns, silver, jewels and diamonds. You name it, he stole it or sold it on for cash, like cattle in South Australia.'

Cattle duffing. I remembered now.

Doreen spoke up. 'That's right. Graham became fascinated by Captain Starlight at the end of last year. It was right after he came back from a weekend with Jimmy's dad in the Outback.'

I pointed to the nugget. 'He brought the gold back around then, I gather. Go on, Barbara.'

'Starlight died a pauper. What if he buried his loot in a cave but something happened? A flood, a rockfall? And what if Graham and his grandpa found it, then Knovak learned about it? Graham may have shown Chuck the nugget.'

'That's a lot of what-ifs, Barbara.' It was Colin.

'Maybe not.' It was Peter. 'I never understood why a bank clerk like Ross would want equipment like picks and shovels and lots of lamps for use underground. He told me it was for a new hobby. Had to order all the goods in especially.'

Mrs L added excitedly, 'And don't forget them stolen explosives.'

I sat down at my desk watching Kyle write it all on the blackboard. Finally Tracey summed it up.

'Impossible as it might seem, it all makes sense. Any idea what type of rock made up the cave, Amy? It might give us a clue where it is.'

I produced the other rock I'd borrowed from Stanley. 'Limestone,' I declared.

Vince came out to examine it.

'Pointed tip. A stalactite from the ceiling of a cave. I used to do some caving. Nearest caves are up in the Warramdandah Ranges, not far from the Murrumbidgee. Proper Outback country.'

'That's not far from my father-in-law's shack, out the back of Mount Mitchell,' Doreen told us.

I looked around at my fellow detectives.

'It makes sense that whatever Chuck and Ross are searching for might be near your father-in-law's home. Maybe they're using Graham to retrieve stuff from the cave if there has been some rockfall that closed it off years ago.'

'Still a lot of what-ifs, Amy, and pretty flimsy evidence,' Kyle reminded us.

Judith returned from the store room. 'Looks like Chuck took the materials for making thermite, potassium cyanide, a few bottles of concentrated acids plus a dozen other potentially explosive chemicals. He was a chemist, after all.'

'What do you think, Doreen?' Kyle asked her.

'Can you send police to the caves? Even if you find their cars, it'll tell us we're on the right track.'

'I agree. I'll organise a team including the local constable to go with me to search that area. Have to be tomorrow, though.'

'Thanks, Kyle. Thanks so much, everyone. You've given me and Jimmy hope. I'll draw you a map of how to get there, Kyle. It's very remote.'

★ ★ ★

When we finished up, I gave the gold nugget to Colin to keep in the school safe. I'd asked Stanley if I could borrow it. Before that, I'd told him how much it was worth based on gold prices in the paper. Colin had told me his family were struggling. Selling that nugget would make a massive difference to their lives.

I was about to leave with the four Levinsons in Vince's Fairlane when Kyle took me to one side.

'Amy. I wondered if you'd care to have dinner with me and Tuesday tonight? We need to talk.'

252

'What about? I'm pretty well bushed.'

'Actually it's about us. And where do we go from here?'

I stared at his expression. It was the same look that was on Keith Connor's face just before he gave me my first proper kiss five years before.

'OK. I accept. I'll tell Mrs and Mr L I'll be home in a few hours. It better be worth it — we were having lamb chops tonight.'

'It will be. There are some things you need to be told before we go any further. And then we'll see if you even want to talk to me . . . ever again.'

12

Kyle's idea of dinner was some strange foreign food called chilli con carne. What was even weirder was that he wanted to serve it with rice.

He insisted he did the cooking, which amazed me. I'd never known a man to do that although, once I thought about it, he didn't have any choice. That was unless Tuesday, the moggy, had some secret talent.

'Have a look around if you want, Amy,' he told me. 'Ignore the odd sock on the floor. I didn't expect company tonight.'

The house was part of the police station. It had three bedrooms but two were empty apart from a bicycle. You could tell a man lived here. The curtains, where there were any, badly needed washing and there were no pictures or photos anywhere apart from one of Kyle in dress uniform with some other police and a few business-suited blokes. I thought I recognised one of them.

'You do realise why we couldn't charge off to find Graham 'til tomorrow?' he called out from the kitchen.

'I couldn't understand Doreen accepting it at first but I think I understand. It's the Outback, isn't it? You people here know it well enough to respect it. It can be dangerous, more so at night.'

'It's a gamble but I'm praying Graham is still needed by them. Ross bought the jellies last week so we can assume he was fine then. Moreover, Ross having Wednesday to Saturday lunchtime away? I'm guessing he was with Graham those days, and not his parents like he told you. Listen, Amy. Can you work that newfangled Facsimile machine? I need to send Doreen's map to Leeton along with the photo of that Knovak guy.'

'Did you say it was a Xerox?'

I heard an expletive. 'Sorry. Damn. Just burned my fingers. Yes, it's a Xerox.'

'I'll try. Is it in your office?'

I'd had training at college on the machines teachers need to use, including Facsimile machines. Frank said 'So simple even a woman can use it' right before I'd stood on his toe.

I went through to where the public came in, surprised to see a cell in one corner. Handcuffs and Kyle's holster hung from an old wooden coat rack, with one leg propped up on a velvet-covered box. I guessed the pistol was somewhere secure.

The photo of my now infamous predecessor and Doreen's detailed map were in the centre of the leather inlaid desk. The Leeton Station phone number was on the cork board.

It took about ten minutes to send it off and get a neatly printed receipt telling me the material had been received. By that time, Kyle had yelled out to tell me dinner was ready. He gave Tuesday her meal on the floor near where we were going to sit. To be honest, Kyle's chilli con carne and Tuesday's canned food appeared remarkably similar. I hoped he hadn't mixed them up.

He'd set the table and two huge bowls of food were steaming in the centre with plates, two forks and napkins waiting. Kyle asked what I wanted to drink. I opted for a cola whereas he chose a beer.

'Not a lover of alcohol,' I explained, feeling a little defensive.

'Help yourself to everything. There's cheese to sprinkle on top if you want.' I stared at the bizarre concoction in front of me. 'Go on, try it. Or are you a coward?'

'I'm no coward,' I said, spooning the chilli onto my plate with the rice on top.

Kyle laughed. 'Wrong way round, but what the heck.' He did the same. 'Dig in.'

The meal was an experience. I'd

never had anything as spicy. Admittedly the cheese toned it down, though I needed another cola by the time we'd finished.

As I went to clear the table he insisted I leave it and sit in the lounge area. He tidied up quickly while I got acquainted with Tuesday. She soon tired of throat scratching and settled on the end of the orange plastic-covered divan.

Kyle came in with another drink for us both. My throat was still on fire from the meal.

'Thanks for the food . . . I think. I guess it's an acquired taste. What would you like to discuss?'

He sat opposite rather than next to me. Right. It was going to be a serious talk.

'This evening proved what I said about you, Amy. You managed to co-ordinate that meeting brilliantly. You have a gift. I was impressed and proud of you both at the same time. Despite your age, you are so mature . . . '

I wasn't used to these many compliments one after the other. It was a teensy bit awkward.

'Most of the time.'

My swollen head quickly deflated. 'Most?'

'Can I assume you fancy me? You intimated that on Sunday night, asking if I *like* liked you.'

I sat up, crossing my arms and legs defensively.

'Sort of.'

'Yet you know nothing about me.'

'That's not true. I know what you do, your age, that you're dedicated and honest.' I didn't tell him that he was pretty good-looking. A girl didn't need to tell a bloke everything.

'But what about my past, my training, why I'm out here in the sticks like you? Are you a virgin?'

Woah, big time. Where did that come from? Even my freckles were blushing.

'Kyle! How dare you! You have no right to ask me that!' I was furious. He smiled.

'I don't want to hear your answer, Amy. You're right. It's none of my business. I simply asked to let you realise I can be abrupt. I'm a copper and there are some bad people out there I must deal with on their terms. Also I have more baggage than you probably do. I'm that much older and . . . ' He took a deep breath. 'And I have been married. I have a daughter whom I visit whenever I can.'

Was he deliberately shocking me? Yes. I could see that now.

'You don't hold back on a young city girl.'

'Life with me isn't going to be a fairytale, Amy. I'm certainly no Prince Charming. You deserve better; some one your own age . . . but not Ross.'

I smiled, in spite of the reality check.

'What's her name? Your little girl.'

'Tamara. She's almost four, going on fourteen.'

The same age as my two sisters.

'Have you ever killed anyone?' It was my turn to take the offensive, to let him realise I wouldn't give up without a fight.

'Yes. In the line of duty. It's part of the reason my marriage didn't work. I found it hard to deal with the memory of what I did. I saved other people but killing anyone, even a criminal, eats away at you inside. Out here, in Gurawang, it helps me cope better. I have a lot of complications already in my life and not everyone might want to share in those, Amy. Probably too much for someone just beginning her own life as a woman.'

When I didn't say anything, Kyle excused himself to finish cleaning up the dishes.

'You stay and think about what I said, Amy. Like I told you earlier you are one fantastic, beautiful young woman who can do much better than a copper in some country town.'

Maybe he was right. I was so confused, emotions and facts running everywhere in my little brain. I remembered that very special first kiss with Keith Connor and how beautiful it had been. I wanted those same thoughts to be there when I first made love, when I married, when my first child would be born.

How could those things be special with a man who had done it all before? Like that tacky song by Barbara Streisand I'd be nothing more than a *Second-Hand Rose*.

On the other hand, he was caring, funny, dedicated, brave; all qualities I admired. He was rugged, muscular and handsome too, reminding me of some of the surfer men I'd liked from afar down at Bondi.

I stood up as Tuesday stretched out on her back and gave a huge yawn before curling up again. That photo I'd seen earlier attracted my attention. Who was that bloke with Kyle? I picked up the picture and squinted at the face I'd half recognised. It was Robin Askin, our state premier and next to him was the Police Commissioner, Norman Allen. They appeared to be presenting a box to Kyle. It looked like the same black box now propping up the wonky coat stand.

'I'll take you home now, Amy,' Kyle called from the kitchen. 'We both have busy days tomorrow.'

'Just a mo, Kyle. I think I left something in your office,' I shouted over clanging of saucepans.

Once I went in, I carefully removed the box from under the leg of the stand. Inside was a medal with a striped ribbon attached. The inscription was *The Queen's Police Gallantry Medal.*

'You are one nosy woman, Amy Shaw. Don't you realise what curiosity did to the cat? Even one as beautiful as you.' Kyle was in the doorway, grinning. 'Don't know how you found out about that. Please put it back where it was.'

'But it should be on display, Kyle. It's . . . it's really important. If it was me, I'd carry it with me all the time; not to boast but just to remind me that other people regard what I've done as special.

Whenever I doubt myself, I'd touch that medal and feel good again.'

'Maybe. But right now it's more useful on the floor. Also, I seriously doubt you'd never have confidence in yourself, Amy. You're perfect.'

'Clearly you don't understand me very well, Kyle. Every day, I look in the mirror and I certainly don't feel perfect. I'm skinny, short, weak and I'm no film star. I rub people up the wrong way because I'm bossy and assertive. On top of that I have freckles. I hate my freckles so much.' I stifled a sob. 'But whoever I am, I force myself to keep going . . . and it's pretty damn hard. If the Premier of New South Wales gave me a medal for bravery, it would make my life so much easier to endure. Even the bloody freckles.'

There was a pause. Finally Kyle spoke.

'Shall we go? It's raining again.'

'OK. As you say, we have a big day tomorrow.'

Inside I was angry at myself for my

latest outburst. It was one thing to feel sorry for myself, but to confess it all to a guy who was a genuine hero? Raving on about my own perceived inadequacies seemed so childish. Engrossed in kicking myself, I missed what he said.

'Sorry. Could you repeat that, Kyle?'

'Nothing important, Amy. I simply said that I love your freckles.'

All that tension was released in an instant. He had said the one thing that I needed to hear.

★   ★   ★

Back at the Levinsons, I wasn't my usual gregarious self. Mrs L noticed it immediately.

'How did it go? Quite a catch, isn't he?'

Without thinking, I replied with a touch of hurt.

'He's already been caught, though. I'm sorry. I shouldn't have — '

'It's OK, Amy. I've met his ex-wife

and little Tamara. It doesn't change who Kyle is.'

'Doesn't it? I wanted my first real boyfriend to be special, not . . . second-hand. And there's . . . '

'The medal? He told me you found it. Said you'd make a brilliant detective.'

'He told you? When?'

'As he was leaving. He loves you, Amy. He simply wanted you to understand that he has a lot of history. When he first came here, he was very confused. When Graham went missing it brought his earlier life back. He received that medal for saving a family from a gunman. Didn't tell you that, did he?'

I was surprised. 'No, he didn't.'

'He shot the other man but was slightly wounded in the gunfight. He saved four people that day. And then you turned up in town.'

I paused. 'Yeah, a brash young woman.'

'Who took control and woke up

everyone with her passion, her determination and own bravery. Can you not understand how much you've altered Gurawang in less than two weeks? Girl. You're the biggest dust-storm this town has ever seen.'

In spite of my feelings I had to snigger.

'As for feeling sorry for yourself because Kyle isn't an innocent like you, learning about life, just think on about the good things that having an experienced partner can give you.'

I thought back to Keith and that first kiss. It might have been mine but it certainly wasn't his. He was teaching me in the same way that I shared my knowledge and experience with my students every day.

Suddenly those swirling storm clouds in my mind were gone. I broke out into a smile.

'Mrs L. How did you ever become so smart when it comes to relationships?'

'Practice, dearie. Now, let's go and watch some telly. *Division Four* will be on in four minutes.'

'I thought you didn't like police shows?'

'Rubbish, Amy. I love them all.'

★ ★ ★

Wednesday morning saw a return to stinking hot sunny days. The DJ on 2RG, the local radio station, told listeners that the rains had gone to wherever rains go before playing Johnny Farnham's *Raindrops Keep Falling on My Head* yet again. I didn't care that it had been number one for weeks. I'd had my share of blinking rain and not just on my head. I switched him off.

I imagined Kyle would be gone already to meet up with the rest of the search team. I only hoped they'd find Graham alive and well.

I was about half way through a morning lesson on the digestive system when the end of period bell rang four times. It was early. That was good. My own stomach was not liking last night's combination of that chilli stuff at Kyle's and ice cream with *Division Four*.

'It's the fire bell, Miss. We have to evacuate!'

Herding the teenagers outside, I searched for flames or signs of smoke. The rest of the school were lining up in the playground with Colin waiting on the veranda overlooking them. He had a microphone in his hand. Kyle was there with him.

Finally we were all assembled quietly.

'Senior Constable Travis has informed me of a possible threat to our town. There's been an attempt to destroy the Burrinjuck Dam on the Murrumbidgee. For that reason, I'm suspending school for today.' There was a cheer from the pupils and one or two teachers. 'The school buses are on their way and Mrs Anderson and others are contacting all parents to either collect you from the school or from bus stops near your homes.' He dismissed the school students.

I nudged one of the other teachers.

'Could you keep an eye on my kids for a mo? I need to see Colin.'

'No probs, Amy.'

Running up to Kyle and Colin, I asked quietly, 'What's going on? We're nowhere near the river — or the dam. Why send the pupils home?'

Kyle answered. 'Amy. At 10.04am, someone tried to blow up the dam with gelignite. It failed.'

'It would. That dam is massive. Wait: gelignite?'

'Yeah. Certainly sounds like our friends. That's why I'm taking no chances with the children. I wouldn't put it past Knovak to punish the school.'

'I can't believe he'd do that.'

'He's probably killed two people already. And don't forget the Railway Hotel. The bloke's totally wacko,' Colin said darkly.

'It doesn't make much sense. They'd realise that the Burrinjuck wouldn't burst. Why do it?'

Kyle pondered a moment. 'A distraction. Every available copper is headed up there.'

'Leaving other, more vulnerable dams or weirs wide open,' I suggested. 'Maybe they're finished with Starlight's cave and want to flood it again. That's how Starlight lost his loot to begin with. When they diverted the water with weirs and dams, the cave probably dried out allowing Jimmy's dad to discover the gold.'

'Makes sense, Amy. You are so smart. So where's the best bet to stop them blowing something else up?' Kyle showed us a map.

Colin pointed to the Gogeldrie Weir past Leeton.

'Destroying that would probably flood the low lying area where the caves are. That is, if we have the location correct. They've probably set up camp near the caves. Shouldn't be too difficult for you coppers to find, now you have an idea.'

Kyle checked with me and I nodded.

'I'll radio it in before I head down there. They need to understand who they're dealing with.'

'Before you go, Senior Constable. Might I have a quick word in private? My lab.'

Kyle followed me into the windowless store.

'Well then. What's so urgent, Amy?'

'This.' I stood on my tippy-toes, locking my arms around his neck, and stretched up to give him a passionate kiss. At first he seemed surprised but quickly joined in.

When we came up for air, Kyle gave me a warm smile. 'That was quite a kiss, Amy. You're sure?'

'I've always been SHAW, Shaw. Now I'm S U R E, sure as well. One hundred per cent.'

'Sounds like my special chilli did the trick.'

'Don't mention the chilli. From now on I'll cook.' I laughed. 'Right, mister, off you go. I love you. Just wanted you to know. Take care — I don't want to lose you now I've found you. One other thing, if you were serious about my freckles.'

'I am.'

'Then you should be aware that they're not only on my face.'

'Oh. That's . . . yes, well that's um . . . interesting.'

I went out to wave him goodbye, then resumed supervising the children as they boarded buses or were collected. After the pub bombing there were no moans about Colin's actions.

Walking home, it hit me. Graham was in more danger today than ever. If Knovak and Ross were tidying up their treasure-hunting operation, then that finality probably included the boy.

What did they say in American cop shows like *77 Sunset Strip*? 'No witnesses.' Flooding the cave would tidy the crime scene up. Why not put Graham in there to share the same fate?

Arriving home, I was surprised to see Peter Gilmore talking to Mr and Mrs L. Moving closer, I realised they were all laughing and behaving like long-lost friends.

'What's happening, everyone?' I asked.

'Some long overdue bridge-building, Amy,' Mrs Levinson conceded. Peter nodded in agreement.

'Better get back to the store, Miriam. See how the girls are coping. I've agreed to make Rhonda manager while I take a back seat for a bit.'

'You? Take it easy?'

'Actually I've had an offer accepted to buy the produce store at West Burumba. It'll be a month or two before I take it over proper. Thought I might wander down to Sydney for a look-see in the meantime. Maybe meet up with an old friend.'

'Does that old friend happen to be female?'

'Early days, Cyril. Like I said yesterday, there's a lot of people I've wronged. What happened to Rhonda ... well, I'm planning on a lot of changes ... for the better. Best be off. Oo-roo.'

'Before you go, Peter.' A question had been niggling me. 'You said Ross purchased a lot of materials from you. Any camping equipment?'

'No. I asked, but he told me he was sorted.'

'Thanks. Take care, Peter.'

'You too, Amy.'

Once he drove off, I explained the situation to Mr and Mrs L.

'We could contact Kyle,' Mrs L suggested.

Easier said than done. None of us had a police band radio. Ringing Leeton Police HQ would be time-consuming. Besides, Kyle was guarding the weir around Coleambally and couldn't abandon that real threat.

'I'll ring Vince. He's in the volunteer fire brigade. They'd have access to the emergency services radio,' Mr L suggested.

It sounded good but I had a feeling time wasn't on our side. Graham was in imminent danger once Knovak and Ross had sabotaged the structures holding back the mighty Murrumbidgee.

'Could I borrow your car, please? I need to see if I can track Graham down. I suspect they've been keeping him at his grandfather's shack.' There wasn't any logic to my decision apart from that lateral thinking thingy that Kyle insisted I had.

'Are you certain you don't want to wait for Kyle? We can organise men to go with you. Joe, Jimmy, Vince. Going by yourself sounds daft, my girl.'

'More than that,' Mr L added. 'It's dangerous.'

'I'll be careful. It's . . . something I have to do. The others can follow. I bet Graham's locked in the shack while Ross and Chuck are off blowing things to pieces. Then they'll do something horrible to him and get away with the treasure.'

'You don't know where the shack is.'

I pulled out the copy of Doreen's sketch that I had drawn at the police station last night.

'I was reading maps since I was little. I could do with a topographical map if you have one.'

Mr L nodded and went to a large drawer.

'You certain, Amy?' Mrs L was concerned.

'I have to try to save Graham. Can I borrow the car, then?'

'Of course, Amy. Just don't take no chances.'

13

The Outback wasn't really a place on a map. It was more of an idea. If you asked any Aussie, he or she would probably say that it's more remote than the Bush, definitely the wrong side of the Black Stump and had the occasional hint of civilisation with towns like Bourke, Humpty Doo and the fictional Woop-Woop.

It wasn't a place most Aussies fancied living in and certainly it wasn't for a city girl like me. One thing you made certain you did when trekking into the Outback was to take plenty of water with you.

The six-cylinder Falcon purred along the Tarmac roads. I was heading west, past Griffith and Yenda in the Murrumbidgee Irrigation Area. The waters diverted from the Murrumbidgee were taken by canal north so that the area was lush and green. Griffith was the wine-growing centre of the state. I wasn't a fan; however it was becoming popular, especially with the snooty sorts on the north shore of Sydney.

Before long I was back in the arid landscape that defined inland Australia. It was becoming more rugged, pastures giving way to jagged hills and ravines not suited for either sheep or wheat.

I took frequent stops to check the map, get my bearings and have a sip of water. There was no air-conditioning in the car so I was really thinking I was driving the world's biggest barbecue.

Radio 2RG was a distant memory, as were the sight of cars or utes that passed me on the road.

It was past one when I turned off the main route onto the driest, dustiest road I'd seen. No rain out here recently. I rolled up the window as clouds of red dust billowed into the air.

Thankfully the track was smoothish as it wound around the hills westward and ever upward. I was keeping a wary eye on the radiator temperature though it remained steady.

There was a T-junction up ahead. No signpost, naturally. Looking both ways it was obvious that left went to nowhere, whereas right led to the back of beyond. Time for a drink and a thorough map check. Compass too.

The topographic inch to two miles map for this area clearly showed the road to the left winding through some very high cliffs. It was one of the notations on Doreen's sketch of the route. *Dead Man's Pass*, she'd cheerfully labelled the narrow passage. It might have been slightly more scary if it was called Dead Woman's Pass, but not much.

The home that used to belong to Jimmy's dad was the other side of the narrow ravine. I could see the intimidating rock faces looming higher as I approached. All I could think of was my favourite Western heroes riding into a similar landscape.

'*What's that up ahead, Tonto?*'

The masked Lone Ranger pointed to a plant festooned with thin slices of smoked pork.

'Ugg, Kemo-Sabe. Very dangerous.'

'Dangerous? Are you out of your wigwam, Tonto? It's just a shrub with meat tied to it.'

'No, Kemo-Sabe. It's a ham-bush.'

On the offchance that this passage might indeed be an ambush I drove slowly up to the narrowest part before accelerating through into a valley enclosed by mountainous peaks. Fortunately, there had been no falling boulders pushed from above; only my heart thumping.

I drove up the track carefully until I could safely pull off the road to park behind a large chunk of fallen cliff-face. If anyone drove in or out, at least they wouldn't spot the car. As for any tyre-tracks, the settling dust would obscure them in seconds.

Although it was approximately one more mile to the structure, I decided to not announce my presence by driving up to the front door. Tonto had taught me quite a lot about being sneaky.

I checked Mr L's knapsack with water, food, knife and compass and slung the binoculars from the front seat around my neck. Reluctantly I left the printed map. I'd dressed for the occasion in khaki shorts and shirt, strong shoes and a cloth hat. My unruly hair was tied back with a bow.

I splashed some Coppertone sun lotion on my exposed skin, for all the good it normally did me. Mum had found some SPF8 in a chemist, the highest they sold. The temperature was probably in the low thirties. Locking the car, I pocketed the keys and clambered up a slope that should allow me to watch the hut for any signs of activity.

There, on the far of the valley, I spied the limestone and wooden structure looking exactly like the sketch on Doreen's map. For fifteen minutes I watched the building and surroundings for any sign of activity using the binoculars.

Nothing appeared to be happening so stealthily I moved around boulders until I was less than a hundred yards away. I listened carefully. Nothing.

Approaching the back door, I could feel my heart beating quickly, my mouth as dry as a drover's dog's. I was positively sick at the thought that somebody might be waiting inside, ready to pounce. Still, I'd come this far.

After pausing for a minute inside, there was still no sound. I could breathe again.

'Anyone there?' I asked.

I heard a whimper from inside a closed room.

'Is that you, Graham?' I called out cautiously.

A child's voice responded, 'Who's there?'

'Friend of your mum, Doreen. Come to get you away from here.'

'No. I have to stay. Go away from me.'

'Graham. You've been kidnapped by

some very bad people. I can save you.'

'I have to stay here. Or they'll hurt my family.'

'Graham. Listen to me. They were lying. Your family will be safe. You're coming with me.'

'Are you positive they're safe?'

'Yes, sweetheart. Hurry up. We have to leave.'

'The door. It's locked. I can't get out.'

It figured. I started rummaging. Finding the key was easier than I expected — it was in a kitchen drawer. Obviously the criminals didn't anticipate a rescue attempt.

Unlocking the door, I had no idea what to expect. Would he be injured, or so traumatised he wouldn't do what I asked? Instead, all I saw was a young boy's face staring at me in wonder.

'Who are you? I don't know you.'

'I'm a new teacher at your school. My name is Amy. Can you walk, Graham?'

'You bet, Amy. Where are we going?'

I looked around the room and the state it was in. 'Away from here, Graham. I have a car. I'm taking you home.'

To be truthful, I was surprised at how healthy Graham appeared. There were the remnants of food all around the room. It seemed Graham had at least been cared for in that respect. His clothing was dirty and torn in places, though he didn't seem as frail as I'd feared.

'Do you know when they'll be back?' I asked him as we dashed from the shelter of the house into the blazing sunlight.

'No. They don't talk to me except to tell me what to do,' Graham replied, running by my side.

'What do you do?'

'Bring the treasure out of the cave for them. The opening . . . it's far too small for them. You're very pretty, Amy.'

We stumbled over some loose stones

as we clambered up a slope. We were making good time back to the car's hiding place.

'Watch out, Amy. Snake.'

I stopped instantly.

'Is it dangerous?' Not that it mattered. It was my practice to avoid snakes of any kind — not that I'd seen many apart from in Taronga Zoo.

'Death adder. Yep. It's deadly. We need to be more careful, Amy.'

As we warily edged around the basking reptile, I asked the boy if he knew much about snakes. I could see the car less than fifty yards away.

'Enough. My grandpa taught me a lot when I stayed out here with him. He's dead, you know.'

'Yes. Your mum told me yesterday. I'm sorry.'

'I miss him a lot. We were going to share the treasure but now . . . ' I could see his emotions breaking through. He'd tried to be brave and strong in front of me . . . a stranger.

I embraced him.

'It's all right, Graham. You're safe now.'

At that moment, I noticed that the front and rear car tyres were flat. A tall, shaggy-haired man with a moustache stepped out from behind a fallen boulder, levelling a rifle at us both.

'You might want to reconsider that last statement, lady. From my point of view you and the brat are totally wrong. In fact — ' He sniggered as he took his sunglasses off. 'You might even say . . . dead wrong.'

14

I stared at the man with the gun, feeling sick that we'd been caught. Charlie — Chuck — Knovak.

His long mousey-brown hair was parted and swept across his forehead, yet it was those beady eyes that were his most distinctive feature.

Even if he were smiling or laughing, those close-set eyes radiated evil to me. Here was a man who would kill without any regrets. Scars curved down one cheek.

'You must be that Shaw bitch. I knew you'd be trouble the first time I saw you in your hotel room. You're younger than I thought. Uglier too. Ross must have been desperate to want you.'

I crossed my arms defiantly. Graham, obviously afraid of Chuck, was standing by my side.

'Says the bloke who could play

Frankenstein's monster with no make-up. Oh, they're scratches — not lines where your face was sewn together.'

He reached up to touch them. I noticed him wince. 'The boy's handiwork. Ended up infected. Could hardly go to a doctor, could I? Still, he doesn't have long to live and nor do you. Get moving. Back to the house. After Ross gets back we'll torch the place.'

Thinking desperately, I manoeuvred him to walk behind us, closer to the snake. There was a loud crack behind us and, for a second, I feared he'd shot one of us in the back. I glanced over my shoulder at the dead snake.

'Better luck next time,' he sneered, reloading the weapon before I could make a move towards him, then aiming the rifle at my head. 'Get going.'

An afternoon wind was gusting now. My hat blew away. I went to retrieve it.

'Leave it. In a few hours, sunburn will be the least of your worries.'

I was already perspiring. I indicated my knapsack of provisions.

'At least some water. Condemned woman, last drink and all that?'

'Fair enough. Drink your water then dump the bag. Hurry up.'

I took two long swigs then offered the plastic bottle to Graham. As he drank, I slipped the covered knife from the canvas bag into my linen blouse and under my belt. I was hoping the two men would be so confident they wouldn't search me. The thought of their hands touching me made me physically sick. I retched onto the sand.

Back at the shack, Knovak shoved us both into the room where Graham had been. It smelled vile. The windows were boarded over from outside.

'Before you go, tell me what this is all about,' I said, as our captor turned to leave.

'Why?'

'To gloat about how clever you are. That's what master criminals love to do, isn't it?'

Knovak grinned. 'So I'm a master criminal all of a sudden, am I?'

'Well Ross hasn't got the brains.' I was trying to appeal to his ego. The more information I could get, the more time I had to be rescued.

'You're dead right there. Ross is an idiot. OK, what do you want me to tell you?' He kept the gun in his hands, ready if I made a move.

'The treasure. You needed Graham to bring it out of the cave?'

'Yeah. A rockfall years ago. Too small an opening for Ross and me. The brat's been bringing it out and now it's all on two trucks. Gold. Over a million dollars worth.'

'Must be heavy. The trucks . . . ?'

'Reinforced. There are jewels and diamonds too — including the Glory Diamond.'

'Never heard of it.'

'You've heard of the Hope Diamond, though.'

My expression told him I had. Taking an object from his jacket pocket, he unwrapped it and held it up. Even in the dim, shuttered room I could see light flashing off its facets. It was less than an inch in size.

'The Glory Diamond is its smaller sister, also found in India. I'll be the richest person in Australia.' He re-wrapped the gemstone before stuffing it back inside the zippered pocket.

'But you stole it. Graham and his grandpa found the cave.'

'Stealing something that had already been stolen by Captain Starlight? I think ownership is a moot point now.'

'Murder isn't. Morag MacAlister? Graham's grandpa?'

'Among others. That's why you both have to die too. Can't have witnesses.'

'The police have photos of you both. They know what you did.' I noticed the grin disappear.

'And judging from your appearance here, I assume they're not far behind.'

I hoped so. Kyle, perhaps others. In retrospect, not waiting for them was a mistake. Another dumb decision which might well have been my last. We'd almost escaped — but almost wasn't good enough, right now.

There was a sobbing noise from Graham.

'You . . . you murdered my gramps?'

'Yes, you pathetic brat. He wouldn't tell me where the gold was. That's why we grabbed you.'

'But . . . but you said . . . '

'I lied. And I would have killed you weeks ago if we'd have been able to enter the cave ourselves. We only kept you fed to keep your strength up, but now we have all the treasure, it's bye-bye.'

Graham wailed.

A car pulled up with three blasts on the horn.

'That'll be Ross. Hopefully Pretty Boy managed to destroy the weir. Flooding the cave will destroy any sign of the treasure or that we took it.'

Ross bounded in, stopping short seeing me.

'Relax, Ross. It's under control. We'll burn this dump with them locked inside. Dead sheilas and brats tell no tales. Did you dynamite the weir?'

Ross nodded, glaring sullenly at me.

'Any trouble?'

'Some copper chased me. I gave him the slip. That Fiat of mine can really move.'

I couldn't resist a jibe. 'You found the keys?'

His move to cuff me was restrained by Knovak.

'Hold on, Ross. I saw something outside — a reflection off glasses or binocs. You positive you weren't followed?' He passed a handgun from his holster to the younger man. 'Cover them. I'll look outside.'

Knovac grabbed his own binoculars and moved to a window. After scanning the horizon he stopped. 'I see him. Police. Heading this way. Thought you told me you lost him, Pretty Boy.'

'I did. He must have guessed I was coming here. And stop calling me Pretty Boy or I'll . . . '

'You'll what? Wimp out again?' Knovak calmly fitted a telescopic sight from one of his other zippered pockets, then propped the rifle on the sill of the open window as he crouched down.

'It's that copper friend of yours, lady. Hope you two weren't attached or nothing.'

In spite of myself, I gasped. Before I could shout a warning, Knovak fired. Once. Twice. Then he stood to remove the sights from the rifle.

'One dead copper.'

'Noooo ... ooo,' I screamed as Knovak picked up a packet of biscuits and began munching.

15

I was beside myself with anger and grief. He'd slaughtered Kyle.

Ross jagged his gun at me as I began to move forward, causing me to pause. Getting us killed now would be pointless. I forced myself to listen to what happened next as it might be important. Inside though, I was drained of any hope. I still couldn't believe any human could be so callous.

'Shall I check if he's dead?' I heard Ross ask.

'No need. I got him in the shoulder, then the heart. I didn't miss.'

'What if he'd radioed it in?'

'I doubt that. These hills are a signal blackspot. How many sticks of gelly do you have left?'

'Two, Chuck.'

'Good. Go up to the top of the pass and blow those boulders we put there.

That'll close it off. We don't want any more unwelcome visitors.'

'And the other?'

'To seal Starlight's cave. Right now, lock them up. I'll get this place ready to torch while you block the road. Get moving, Pretty Boy. Won't be long now and we'll be super-rich.'

'Sounds good, Chuck. I owe that girl a lot of payback. Hold on, what about my car? With the canyon blocked I can't drive it out.'

'You can buy a hundred cars if you want. We'll hike over the ridge to the trucks and the cave then get going before nightfall.'

Ross slammed the door and locked it. All my bravado vanished as I collapsed on the bed in tears. It was Graham's turn to comfort me. When my anguish faded enough for me to consider our continuing predicament, I lay debating our best options to escape death by fire.

I still had the knife. Making certain it wouldn't be seen if the door was opened quickly, I fingered the blade as I planned when to use it.

'Graham. They're going to burn us alive unless we do something.'

'But they both have guns, Amy.'

'We don't have many options. If only we could convince them to take us outside, we'd possibly have a chance to get away.'

'It'd be better if they put us in Starlight's cave when they dynamite it shut.'

'Better? To die from no food or being drowned when it fills up with water? How's that better?'

'Listen.' He leaned over. Once he'd finished, I could see we had a chance if they took us there.

'How far is the cave from here?'

'About a mile. Over the southern ridge and down the bottom on the other side. That's where they parked the trucks. But how are we going to change their minds, Amy? We can hardly ask them to kill us somewhere else.'

'We can if we're smart. Here's what to do.'

Tonto taught me about sneakiness. Mum taught me about subterfuge.

★   ★   ★

About an hour later the two men opened the door. I'd heard the thunder of the gelignite exploding and the landslide of rocks that followed. Tonto's narrow ambush pass was presumably completely blocked.

Ross waved us out with his hand gun. I sighed.

'Come on. What are you waiting for? Light the match, leave us to burn. Get it over with.'

Knovak came over to us, scowling irritably.

'Why are you so eager to die here?' he asked.

'I just am. Hurry it up.'

Knovak glared at Graham. 'Why's she behaving like this? What's she scared of?'

'I don't know,' the boy snivelled.

'Tell me or so help me, after I kill you

299

two, I'll go back to that dump of a pub and kill your family. I'll make your bratty sister watch and kill her last.'

'No. Please . . . I'll tell you. When I explained about the cave, Amy freaked out. She said she can't stand small spaces. Even the thought of being trapped scares her.'

'Did she now? Imagine that. Missy High and Mighty being scared of tight spaces. Death by burning here might be too good for them. Drowning or starving sounds much more delicious, especially if the girl is a blubbering idiot.'

Ross smiled. 'Yeah. Payback time, bitch.'

Knovak gloated too.

I spat at Graham, making certain that I missed him. 'You stupid kid. Why did you tell them?'

He cowered. 'I had to. They threatened to kill my family. At least they'll be safe now. I'm sorry.'

Knovak sneered, before addressing Ross. 'We agree, then. After all the grief and scratches that brat has given me, and the hassles the ginger gave you, I reckon a long, lingering death in Starlight's cave would be much more satisfying.'

Ross nodded, just like one of those plastic dogs on a car's back shelf. 'We could wound them and still put them in the cave.'

'Do you want to lug them up that hill? I don't. Course I could give you fifteen minutes alone with her beforehand, if you want.'

I shuddered at the prospect.

'Naw. Look at the state of her.'

I didn't know whether I should be grateful or insulted. In this case Ross had avoided me stabbing him . . . at least for the moment.

He was right about one thing. I was a mess. The sun lotion had done little to protect my delicate complexion. The backs of my hands and arms were fuchsia pink. The loss of my sunhat hadn't helped. I had a terrible headache from the heat and the thought of Kyle being dead, as well as their plans for us, was tearing me up inside.

'Move it,' commanded Ross. Once outside we paused while Knovak poured petrol over the basic furniture and wooden kitchen, finishing up with a fluid trail outside. He struck a match and threw it. With a whoosh the building became a blazing inferno, searing the already stifling air around us.

'Ladies and brats first,' Knovak declared with a snide chuckle. 'Head straight up the hill.'

I turned to see if Kyle's body was visible. He'd been shot on the road side of the shack, and the flames danced in between where he probably lay and our present path. I couldn't spy him. The late afternoon sun was directly ahead of us so I shielded my eyes as I trudged along, occasionally skidding backwards on the gravel slope.

When we crossed the ridge, keeping our footing on the downhill side was even more difficult. I took dainty steps side on, fighting to keep my balance. The others were also struggling, with dust stinging our eyes. Eventually I made out two trucks parked near a dark hole in the facing cliff side. Other depressions or caverns in the worn limestone rock face were visible giving the creamy landscape an almost pocked appearance.

As we passed the covered trucks, Knovak took his jacket off and threw it into one of the cabs. He assumed there was no one around to steal it and he was sweating like a pig from the arduous hike.

I was relieved once we clambered up a short slope into the cool shade of a cavern mouth. It took a few moments for my pupils to adjust. Containers of gold were stacked in the shade.

'You know the way, brat. Get walking.'

Graham donned a miner's helmet and began to scramble through a crevice, climbing some rockfall to a hole above. I pretended to panic and fought to stay out of the fissure but Ross shoved me in, pointing his gun.

'Do they need the lights? The kid's brought all the gold out.'

'Better if they can see their tomb after we blow the opening. Besides, Amy here might like to see the skeletons of Starlight's men; the ones he murdered to protect the secret location.' He laughed with a deep guffaw.

I played along, begging him not to make me go into the cavern. He lost his temper, shoving us towards the narrow fissure among the fallen boulders. The rockfall extended to the roof of the huge space.

With every step I took towards that Stygian abyss, I pretended it terrified me more. Part of it wasn't play-acting, though. I prayed that Graham's revelation about the cave's interior wasn't some childhood fantasy.

I started to shake and scream as I was forced further into the blackness.

Watching our footing as we passed

from muted daylight to darkness was petrifying. If Graham hadn't assured me it was safe, I would have dreaded the cavern roof tumbling down on us.

'I've done it hundreds of times, Amy,' he whispered. 'The limestone seems to have stuck together since Starlight's time. Just watch the bumpy floor. You'll have to scrunch up real small to fit through.'

He was right about the tight fit. My plaintive cries continued for the benefit of our captors. I had visions of getting stuck, unable to move. If it hadn't been for Graham's verbal prodding, I might still have been in that tiny passage when they dynamited the entrance closed.

'Come on, Amy. You're almost through.'

All I could see ahead was the light from my lamp and Graham's own head lamp. Finally I could sense the tiny gap widening. Peering back, there was a distant light from the outside.

'How far have we come?' It felt like

ages of crawling and squeezing. We kept our voices low so the men couldn't hear us, though it seemed they were too busy preparing their escape.

'About ten feet. They think it's much longer and narrower.' His face appeared in front of mine. 'That Mr Knovak ain't the only one who can lie.'

I understood now that Graham had survived this long by prolonging his importance.

'I'm guessing you pretended that it was very hard to find and retrieve the treasure too. Yeah?'

'You bet. Most of the gold is here, just in front. I told them it was way inside. Did I do good?'

'You certainly did, Graham. We'd better get further in. We don't want to be caught by falling rocks when they seal the entrance.'

The cavern had opened up considerably. Graham disappeared for a moment then the cave came to life, as he switched on a number of lights that were obviously already there.

'Wow,' was all I could say. Stalagmites climbed from the floor and a mirror image of stalactites adorned the fifty-foot ceiling like gigantic raindrops captured on some three-dimensional photo. The roof pulsed with darkened flutters of grey.

'Bats. They live here during the day. That's how I found the secret. I followed them.'

Graham was intent on sharing the mysteries and wonders of his prison for two months. Instead of blindly following the threats and demands of his captors, he had discovered his own sanctuary in here — far from their reach.

I made out a horizontal line many feet above us. Graham noticed my gaze.

'Gramps reckoned Starlight hid his loot in here but there was some sort of earth movement that closed the entrance and flooded the cave. When they built the dams around the time he was born, the cave dried out.'

'Knovak mentioned skeletons?'

In the light shining upwards from the battery lamps, I could see Graham pointing like Death himself. Jumbled bones lay on the floor towards the other end of the cathedral-sized space.

'There were three. All shot here.' He tapped his forehead. 'The treasure was in those chests.'

My reverie was interrupted by echoey sounds from outside.

'We'd better get away from this part, Graham. Quick.' Between us, we grabbed as many of the lamps as we could and began weaving through the stalagmites, scattered bones and rubble.

Light glistened back at us from the ground.

'That water. It wasn't here before,' Graham mentioned in passing. The cave was filling with water once again, thanks to Ross' destruction of the Murrumbidgee weir.

'Careful with the limestone spikes, Amy. Some are sharp. Here, use these.' He passed me gloves like the ones he was wearing.

'You're well stocked, Graham.'

'If I said I lost something, they'd give me more. They needed me to fetch the gold. Head for Mr Spooky up there.'

'Mr Spooky?'

Again he pointed. I could see a ghostly outline made by crevices in the rocks. The water was rising visibly now. In those telly shows where the hero was trapped in a cave, he always had smooth ground underfoot. This place was so hard to navigate. I put my weight on a stalagmite, only to stumble when it snapped off. One of my lamps fell into the bubbling stream and fizzled out.

Behind us, there was a rumble followed by crashing and a cloud of dust that momentarily blinded us. The bats circled frantically, disturbed by the explosion, before darting like a scary gust of leaves past our heads and towards Mr Spooky.

It was the other exit; the one Graham told me about in his gramp's shack. If Ross or Knovak had any idea it existed, they could have stripped the cave weeks before. There'd have been no reason to keep Graham alive.

'It's a steep climb and it's up very high. But I fixed a rope to help us.'

I was impressed and told him so. 'But why didn't you escape?' I inquired. Then I remembered. The murderers threatened his family. He might be one of the cleverest boys I'd met, but he was still a child trusting what he was told by any adult.

A glance behind confirmed the cave was filling up fast. By the time we reached the ledge, every part of my sunburned body was aching. I hadn't eaten since breakfast and was feeling crook.

We had to keep going. The passage wasn't narrow, yet it was windy and difficult to walk along in my sandshoes.

'You 'kay, Amy? Not much further.'

I fingered the knife hilt inside my blouse. Even if we got out of the mountain, where could we go? Could we steal the truck? I doubted it. So that meant walking out, but I had no idea where to go. There were no roads around apart from the one they'd drive out from.

One thing at a time. Get outside first. 'There it is. See the daylight?'

The literal light at the end of the tunnel. Graham and I struggled though overhanging vegetation out into the early dusk. It took a while before my eyes adjusted. We'd made it this far.

'What now, Amy?' Graham asked. He'd done his share, found a way out. Now it was up to me.

The trouble was that I was feeling very ill now. I suspected trudging through the arid landscape earlier, unprotected from the harsh sun, had been too much for me. Added to that was the mental and physical exhaustion of the drama. Kyle was dead. The crooks were getting away. I'd found Graham but he was far from being rescued.

We'd exited onto a space about ten feet by ten, a limestone ledge gradually sloping away on the left to the base below. The other side was a sheer fall of thirty feet.

I gazed out across the vista of scrub and sparse trees. Despite knowing the setting sun was in the north-west, it wasn't any use to me. I couldn't concentrate or remember the topographic map. I didn't have a clue where any towns or roads were. Collapsing onto a rock, I stared blankly from the ledge on which we were sitting.

'Which way, Amy? Which way?'

'I don't know, Graham.' I replied, weakly. 'I think we're lost.'

16

Graham sat mutely as I took deep, gasping breaths. I had to make a decision. Night was closing in and we needed to set off. Or would it be better to stay here at the cave? I noticed Graham shivering and realised I was also. The Outback's temperature was dropping quickly.

From our left, I heard an engine start, then move a bit before idling. The trucks getting ready to leave? Were we that close? They must have been around the corner of the cliff-face.

I had a plan at last. A totally daft plan, but one thing at a time. What if I could grab a map from the truck? It would be dangerous but the light was fading quickly and I had the element of surprise. They thought we were trapped in Starlight's cave.

'Wait here.' I struggled to my feet,

almost collapsing as my right knee gave way. Of all the days for it to play up. Now it would swell, and I'd find walking more and more painful. Nevertheless I had some time before that happened.

Shivering and reluctant, Graham agreed. I set off warily in the direction of the engine noises. It seemed Ross and Knovak were still loading. They'd parked the trucks facing the cave entrance and switched on the lights.

I kept to the shadows, reaching the first truck cabin and opening the door. I saw nothing of use, even in the glove box. Then I heard Ross calling out as he pushed a trolley to the other truck.

Ross. The man who tried to seduce me and probably punctured the Levinsons' petrol tank. That gave me an idea. As he walked back to the cave, I took out the knife and nicked the fuel line slightly; just enough to cause a slow leak.

Moving across to the other truck, I did the same. The trucks wouldn't get far but at least they'd be able to drive away, giving Graham and me some breathing space.

On impulse, I grabbed Knovak's jacket for warmth and hobbled back to Graham.

It was almost night; dusk was very rapid. I told him what I'd done and decided we'd be more protected back just inside the passageway we'd escaped through. The wind was strong and cool. There, we'd be less exposed and with Knovak's jacket between us, slightly warmer.

We heard the trucks depart soon after, their headlights barely visible from our shelter. Crickets and cicadas took up a chorus between them, bats and owls flew nearby and Aussie animals came out to forage, joined by rats, mice and rabbits.

Once or twice I was roused by something nipping my bare leg. I scrunched up tighter next to Graham, only half registering the glow from a light in the distance.

'You awake, Amy?' Graham whispered. 'There's something in this pocket.' He lifted it out and shone a torch on it.

'It's the Glory diamond!' I said, suddenly wide awake. 'Douse the light and be quiet.'

At first there were no sounds that weren't natural. Then we heard the crunch of footsteps. Knovak. I cursed myself for forgetting he'd put the diamond in the zipper pocket.

I'd figured he wouldn't be too bothered about a missing jacket and would drive off with Ross, both of them running out of fuel somewhere away from here and civilisation.

What I hadn't counted on was the diamond. No way would Knovak overlook that. He must have stopped as soon as he realised it had been taken and that we must have done it.

'Hey you two,' Knovak shouted from below. 'I know you're out there, hiding. I'm going to find you and make you both wish you were dead.' He went on to shout about the torture he intended to inflict on us. The guy had one sick imagination. Graham was shivering in fright.

'Maybe we should give it back. He might let us go,' he whispered in my ear.

'No way. He tried to kill us once today. I don't think he'll change his mind. Our best bet is to wait and make our way out of this area tomorrow. If we try to leave now, he'll see our lamps and it's too dark to move without them. Just try to sleep. I'll wake you, first thing at dawn.'

Reluctantly he agreed. Knovak, his torch and his rantings were moving further away. I settled down to try and sleep but my leg was too painful. I lay awake, trying to stay alert. It was going to be a long night.

★ ★ ★

'Wake up, Amy. You've been bitten.'

It took a moment to register where I

was and who was speaking. Then I remembered.

It was dawn. Graham was brushing madly at my ankles. 'Bull ants.'

Suddenly I could feel them crawling over my skin. The black and orange insects could be up to an inch long and were vicious little beggars.

I stood up to clear the last of them away as did Graham. My legs had been bitten all over, the venom stinging like mad. Then I saw their nest near the edge of the ledge. Hundreds of them were swarming around searching for food.

'Here. Rub this on,' said Graham, handing me some bracken fern from near the cave entrance. 'Gramps taught me.'

I did as he suggested, surprised that it helped. At the same time I became aware of how swollen and sore my knee was. No way could I walk out, especially with trigger-happy Knovak on the prowl.

I showed Graham my knee and

explained he'd have to go himself, moving as quietly as he could away from where we could just see Knovak's truck and him pacing around it.

He seemed more confident in finding his way to some town that he said was about fifteen miles away where his grandfather went for provisions.

'Last night it was too dark to see proper but if I follow the creek over there, it'll help.'

He helped me over to sit in the shade by the cliff-face. The ant nest was about six feet away but they didn't seem to be foraging near me.

'See you soon,' I told Graham.

'You too, Amy. I'll bring help as soon as I can.' We peeked through the bushes but couldn't spot Knovak anywhere. His truck was still there.

'Better go,' I told Graham, fearing Knovak was heading this way. Within seconds he had disappeared. I'd given him as much help as I could about staying out of sight and being quiet.

Bushes rustled below me. It was

Knovak at the base of the cliff, about two hundred yards away and eighty feet down. He had his rifle in his hand.

Graham darted between cover. Knovak was heading straight for him. There was nothing I could do. Or was there?

I grabbed a handful of gravel and tossed it over the ledge. Knovak stopped and turned. I remained hidden in the shadows and bushes.

'That you up there?'

I didn't answer what had to be the stupidest question I'd heard in my entire life.

Nevertheless he was coming to investigate. Graham was making faster progress now he knew where Knovak was. In a moment he was out of sight completely.

When I tried to edge back into the cave, I had to give up. My knee was a real problem. All I could do was wait as the murderer clambered up the slope towards me, his head appearing scant feet from me as he reached the flattened area.

'Don't know how you got out, Amy, but it won't do you any good now.' He stayed well back from my feet, edging round to see the cave opening.

'It's always been there. You and Ross could have entered Starlight's cave any time you wanted. Quite a pleasant stroll to get up here.'

His face twitched. Graham had made a fool of him for almost two months. I forced myself to shuffle to one side. Knovak moved also, careful of the precipice edge. He pointed the rifle at me.

'Where's my diamond?'

I held it out in my hand, dropping it by my side. He took a tiny step to his left.

'Guess it's time for you to die. Say hello to your copper friend when you see him.'

I turned my head slightly, staring straight ahead. 'Hello, Kyle.'

17

Knovak paused. It was just the delay I needed. The bull ants that had been aggressively swarming up his legs from the moment he'd stood on their nest had reached his bare skin.

He yelped as they plunged their stingers into his flesh. His gun fired into the air as he jumped from one foot to the other. Seizing the moment, I threw myself towards him, almost fainting from the agony in my knee. The knife plunged into his calf. As he staggered, his arms began windmilling.

It was too late. Charles Knovak fell over the ledge, screaming. I pulled myself to the edge. His body lay sprawled on rocks thirty feet below. He wouldn't be getting up.

Groaning, I pulled myself back to my spot. The Glory Diamond glistened in the morning sun. I wrapped it and placed it my blouse pocket. If I was going to die here, at least I'd die rich.

I thought of Kyle. I'd pretended he was alive to distract Knovak. At least I'd had revenge on his killer. I sagged, closing my eyes. The pain was duller and sleep seemed a good idea. If only I could have a drink. A milkshake would be good.

I was only dimly aware of the shadows disappearing as the sun beat down. My face itched so I dragged my hand up to touch my cheek. It hurt. Hopefully the ants had better things to do than attack me again. I was drifting, reliving the nightmare of the last two days.

'Kyle,' I called out in my delirium.

'I'm here, Amy,' he replied from far away. I struggled to see him yet all there appeared was a blinding white light.

'You can't be. You're ... you're dead.'

'I'm not dead, Amy.' I saw his hazy face and a hand reaching out to touch my face.

'Don't,' a woman said, harshly. 'The sunburn.'

'S'at you, Judith? Wha . . . '

'Don't speak. Sip this.' A shadow blocked the light and the heat. I opened my eyes again. There were so many faces staring back. Peter, Vince, young Graham, Joe, Doreen . . . and Kyle, one arm in a makeshift sling. They all appeared shocked at my appearance.

'Guess I *really* messed up my lippy this time,' I half-joked. And then it all went dark.

⋆ ⋆ ⋆

I woke occasionally during the next twenty-four hours. One time was on a stretcher being carried. I recall an ambulance and a hospital theatre, then Mum and Dad being by my side.

It was two days before I was aware enough to converse properly. I felt like a mummy with so many dressings. Surprisingly, there was no pain. Drugs, someone told me. I'd pieced together a lot of what happened; from conversation between hospital staff or my many visitors and family.

Mum and Dad were there on one side of the bed, Kyle and Mrs L on the other.

'Is Knovak dead?' I asked.

'Yes.' Kyle was speaking. 'The townsfolk found me first. Then we tracked down Graham with Joe's help. He'd been wandering in circles. His story was pretty fantastic but it was believable enough for police to track down Ross. There were a few shots fired but he gave himself up quickly enough. His truck broke down about ten miles from the cave. A cut fuel line. Your doing?'

I nodded. My throat still hurt. 'The treasure?'

'All recovered, including that giant sparkler in your pocket. Some very amazed government people, plus historians. And before you ask, Graham's family are getting a substantial reward. Very substantial.'

'Can't believe you're alive, Kyle.

Knovak was certain he killed you.' I smiled at him, noticing the bandages around his upper arm. At least the sling had gone.

'I'm glad. If he'd checked I wouldn't have been so lucky. It was you who saved me, you know.'

'Me? But how?'

Kyle lifted his medal case from his breast pocket. It was shattered, revealing a deeply dented medal inside. He grinned.

'It was your suggestion to carry it with me. As good as those lightweight bullet-proof vests they're trying to perfect.'

'I hope they'll give you a replacement.'

'I dunno. I feel this one means so much to me already.' He opened his shirt to show me the bruising.

I turned to Mrs L. 'I'm so sorry about your car.'

'Oh, don't be, Amy. We got it back, all fixed up courtesy of Peter. It seems that Ross fella wasn't as good at blowing up that narrow pass as he thought. Now if you'll excuse me, I have to go see how my husband's getting on with that cataract operation. He's such a baby when it comes to needles. We'll see you home soon, Amy.'

'Give my love to Mr L, please.'

She gave me a kiss on my bandaged forehead.

'I'll join you, Mrs Levinson,' said Kyle. 'Then it's off to see my bosses. You would not believe the paperwork your little rescue attempt has caused me.' His goodbye kiss was on the lips.

Mum, and Dad moved their chairs closer. Dad was first to speak. I expected a lecture.

I wasn't disappointed.

'Amy. Don't ever scare us like that again.'

Mum came to my defence. 'She can't help getting into trouble, Paul. It's those adventure genes she inherited from you. You can't stop our little girl from helping people and standing up for what she believes in. It'd be like asking a kangaroo not to hop.'

'I realise that, Anne.' Dad broke out in one of his cheeky grins. 'Bad news or good news first about that pretty face of yours?' It was a game we'd played all my life.

'Good news, Dad.'

'You'll be as beautiful as ever in a week or so. The sunburn's superficial.'

I smiled. 'Bad news?' I expected some comment about the ant stings.

'You'll still have those freckles you hate.'

My equally freckled mum punched him playfully.

'Actually, Dad. I kinda like my freckles now.'

'That Kyle bloke? Sweet on you, is he? He seems like a decent man. We had a good talk about car rallies. He knows more about me than I do myself. Even asked for my autograph.'

Mum chirped in. 'You sure that wasn't for some statement, Paul?'

Dad shrugged, then became serious. 'Your mum and I were concerned about you being so far from Sydney but with the number of your new friends we've met, we've decided you'll be fine.'

'Better than fine,' said Mum, giving me a gentle hug. 'Some children left you flowers and cards. So many cards.'

'I know.' There were over a hundred from adults and students alike. 'The doctors said I could go home Monday. By 'home', I mean . . . '

'We understand. Gurawang is your new home.'

⋆   ⋆   ⋆

On Monday, Kyle collected me in his police Monaro. I was not feeling great but each day saw an improvement. The ant stings were a distant memory and my last shred of burned skin had flaked off. It would be good to resume work soon.

Driving up from Leeton District Hospital, Kyle glanced at the notepad on which I was writing.

'What have you got there, Amy?'

'My Never Again list. In no particular order; going to sleep near an ant nest, having a gun pointed at me, searching for a kidnapped person, thinking you were married to a cat, oh . . . and getting sunburned.'

'All very sensible. How's that knee of yours?'

'Ripper. No pain, no swelling. Judith, Doreen and Barbara have drawn up a timetable to help me and the Levinsons for the time being. I gather Judith secured that district nurse job thingy — hey, this isn't the way to the Levinsons'.'

'Have to go somewhere first. Won't be long.'

He drove past the school. There was no one around. Typical day in Gurawang.

'Your dad told me you always wanted to ride in a police car with the siren on.'

I laughed. 'Yeah. When I was ten.'

'So you don't want to flip that toggle switch?'

'Well . . . ' Giggling, I reached out to

press it. Immediately the siren blared and there were flashing lights everywhere. 'Wow! This is great.'

Kyle turned onto the main street, slowing to a crawl.

'What the . . . ' Hundreds of people were cheering and waving, some holding up placards saying *Welcome Home Amy*. I was amazed. I waved back, tears filling my eyes.

'I have to get out.'

'You sure? You're not to exert yourself.'

'I'll only be a minute. Please?'

It was more like ten. Kyle and Doc MacAlister bundled me back into the car when I almost passed out from the effort of trying to thank the crowd. Kyle passed me a microphone and we continued driving with my squeaky, emotional voice resounding from the police cruiser's loudspeaker.

'It was fantastic. I never suspected.'

'You're our heroine, Amy,' the doc said as we turned into Kookaburra Road.

I saw the Levinsons' Falcon parked on the drive — along with a white Fiat 850 coupé. I felt my blood pressure rising.

'Why is Ross' car there?'

Kyle answered. 'Technically it wasn't Ross' car. It belonged to the bank. And now, after a bit of discussion with the new manager, it belongs to you — along with free lifetime insurance.'

'Golly, gee, wow. My own car. I want to take it for a drive.'

The doc spoke up. 'Not for a few days, young lady. Doctor's orders.'

'Doctor's orders. All I've heard for days. You're right of course.'

'I'll hold onto these for a few days, Amy.' Kyle held up the Fiat keys. 'Don't want you throwing them away again.'

'No chance of that, Senior Constable . . . sir.' I gave him a kiss as Mrs L, Doreen and Judith stepped out of Judith's car that had pulled up behind us.

'Let's get you inside, Amy. I need to

check those dressings,' said Judith.

'Yes, nurse,' I replied with a smile.

★ ★ ★

After dinner I felt much better. I was surprised when Kyle arrived with a dossier of papers.

'I realise it might be a bit much for you, Amy, but I could do with some assistance . . . from all of you. These thefts have me stumped.'

Mrs L checked with me and I nodded. Tracking down a thief was not on my Never Again list. Kyle spread the folders out on the table.

'In the last week there have been a dozen items stolen from local farms, weird stuff that doesn't make sense.'

I kicked our investigation off. 'First things first, Senior Constable. We have a thief so we need a code name . . . Mr L?'

Mr L's eye operation had been a complete success. He smiled at me. 'We call him Ned, after Ned Kelly.'

'Could be a woman. Nedina? Men don't normally steal jewellery,' Mrs L added, scanning the missing goods list. 'I'll stick the kettle on.'

'Sorry,' said Kyle. 'Isn't *Division Four* on tonight? You all like that show, don't you?'

'We have fifty minutes till it starts. You can watch it with us if you want, Kyle,' Mrs L offered.

'Could I? I've never watched it before.'

I winked at him. 'Good. You might learn something about proper police work. Now let's check those documents.' We all began reading, chatting and making notes of salient points.

Fifty minutes to solve a baffling crime? Nedina-blinking-Kelly didn't have a chance.

We do hope that you have enjoyed reading this large print book.

Did you know that all of our titles are available for purchase?

We publish a wide range of high quality large print books including:
Romances, Mysteries, Classics
General Fiction
Non Fiction and Westerns

Special interest titles available in large print are:
The Little Oxford Dictionary
Music Book, Song Book
Hymn Book, Service Book

Also available from us courtesy of Oxford University Press:
Young Readers' Dictionary
(large print edition)
Young Readers' Thesaurus
(large print edition)

For further information or a free brochure, please contact us at:
Ulverscroft Large Print Books Ltd.,
The Green, Bradgate Road, Anstey,
Leicester, LE7 7FU, England.
Tel: (00 44) **0116 236 4325**
Fax: (00 44) **0116 234 0205**

Other titles in the
Linford Romance Library:

A YEAR IN JAPAN

Patricia Keyson

When ex-librarian Emma announces she's accepted a year-long position to teach English in Japan, the news shocks her grown children. Enjoying single life after half a year of estrangement from her husband Neil, Emma can't wait to embark upon her adventure in three weeks. Then Neil is hospitalised after a car accident, and needs a carer at home while he recovers. Emma is the only one available to help. Three weeks — can Neil make up for lost time before Emma leaves, and will she let him back into her heart?

GRANDPA'S WISH

Sarah Swatridge

Melanie is growing tired of her job at a family law firm, until she is tasked with tracing a Mr Davies, the beneficiary of a late client's estate. Tracking him down, Melanie is surprised to find Robbie-Joe uninterested in the terms of the will, especially when he learns that it belonged to a grandfather he had no idea existed. To claim his fortune, Robbie-Joe must complete twelve challenges in twelve months. But Melanie has a challenge of her own: to stop her feelings for Robbie-Joe becoming anything more than professional . . .

HOME TO MISTY MOUNTAIN

Jilly Barry

UK-born Hayley Collins is visiting Australia, staying with a friend and looking for work. Craig Maxwell runs a holiday resort at Misty Mountain, a four-hour drive from Melbourne. When Hayley applies to be an administrator at the resort, Craig takes her on — and much else besides. She has to return to England in twelve months. He's engaged to a woman whose father is helping to keep the resort's finances in the black. So when Hayley and Craig fall in love, it seems a future together is only a distant dream . . .